The City Trap

The City Trap

John Dalton

TINDAL STREET PRESS

First published in 2002 by
Tindal Street Press Ltd
217 The Custard Factory, Gibb Street, Birmingham B9 4AA
www.tindalstreet.org.uk

Typesetting: Tindal Street Press Ltd

A CIP catalogue reference for this book is available from
the British Library.

ISBN 0 9535895 6 0

Printed and bound in Great Britain by
Biddles Ltd, Woodbridge Park Estate, Guildford.

To K and L

Acknowledgements

Thanks to Myra; and to Joel, Emma and Alan at Tindal Street Press for their help and support.

1

'I mean, look at this! What is going on?'

'Seems like we're stuck.'

'Stuck, yeh, like every day it gets quicker to walk! Bleedin crazy!'

'Hold on, that bloke's letting you in.'

'Thank the fuck you!'

Scobie Brent nudged his car into the crawling traffic of the main road. It was half a mile bumper to bumper ahead of him. Once in the flow, he sighed and wiped imaginary sweat off his brow. Then he smiled reassuringly at the woman who sat next to him.

'Bloody nation's grinding to a halt,' Claudette muttered.

'Yeh, even in our business we have schedules to meet.'

'Reckon we'll make it?'

'Plenty of time . . .'

Scobie hadn't meant to cuss out loud. 'Keep your lid on,' the boss had said. 'Be smarmy.' Huh, as if Scobie couldn't handle a bird like Claudette. This job was a piece of piss. He worked his thumbs into the ribs of the steering wheel, pressed hard and then grinned as they paled with the pressure.

'Anyway, Scobie, you got any plans to get out of this dump?'

'Don't know, luv, I ain't the kind to make plans. You know, take each day as it comes.'

'Wow . . .'

There was little point in keeping an eye on the road. Scobie looked in the rear-view mirror, smoothed back his hair and then cast a frank gaze over Claudette.

OK, quite tasty, he thought. Worthy of a second look . . . unlike the rest of the slags. Then he put on a casual smirk and let his eyebrows float.

'You got plans then, have you, sweetheart?'

'Too right.'

'You gonna give me an idea?'

'I don't reckon you'd know what I was on about.'

The car nudged forward a few feet at a time. What a flesh creeper, she thought, real dangerous scum. But Claudette reckoned she was used to it, wits and instincts finely tuned to treading the thin line of hassle avoidance. She looked out of the window. The last of daylight had finally gone and city light had taken over. This sudden tilt from day to night seemed to bring more movement in the traffic and Scobie could accelerate down the main street, his leering presence in the car feeling less oppressive. Claudette liked car-cruising in the city. It seemed to her the only way such a place made sense. You could be everywhere and anywhere and somehow feel part of the godawful sprawl. *Don't clog up on me yet, keep moving. Movement is desperately needed, thank you very much.*

She leaned back in her seat and felt the thrust of speed. *Fingers crossed, one big deal and I'll be over the horizon and gone for good.* Then she smiled at the neon shop signs and imagined the envious thoughts of friends who would wonder how she got away.

'We're using the Varna pad tonight,' Scobie drawled, feeling more relaxed and in the groove of his work.

'Bit down-market, isn't it?'

'It's what the bloke wants.'

'What sort of jerk is it this time?'

'Fuck knows, insurance or something.'

'Don't know how the boss manages to find such well-heeled shits.'

'Cos he knows where they crap, of course!'

Scobie gave out a braying laugh and ignored the grimace that Claudette made. He began to soothe the car through darkened backstreets, skirting empty acres of flattened factories and keeping his eyes alert for signs of police.

'Do I have to do anything funny?'

The nerves. Always just before, Claudette felt the nerves tighten her mouth and make her stomach queasy.

'Nah . . . just be your professional self.'

'Anything else lined up for me?'

'You know the boss . . . Shit, who knows when he'll pull out a golden egg?'

'Yeh, well, he certainly likes his hand up the arse of a bird.'

Scobie parked his car at the rear entrance of Varna Court. He looked up at the three-storey building with its grey bricks and saw that everything was quiet. He grabbed a large sports bag out of the boot and then took Claudette by the arm to the entrance. The flat looked obviously unlived in, but it was furnished respectably and didn't come over as a knocking shop. Scobie moved straight into the bedroom and began to unzip his bag. He saw his face in the large mirror above the headboard and he grinned uneasily at himself. Why am I on edge? he then thought. Cos the damn bird is getting to me, that's why. His fingers fumbled for a bottle of Scotch.

'This place is done out all right.'

'Seen one, seen em all.'

'Yeh, but you said the punter wanted something down-market. This looks more like home from home.'

'What the fuck do you know about how rich pricks live?'

'Well I was –'

'Just shut up and take your clothes off!'

'Why do I have to do that?'

'Because I've got some special kit in this bag. What the bloke ordered, see!'

'All right, keep your hair on.'

God, Claudette thought, I'll be glad when this one's out the way.

But that was the way she'd been feeling with all the tricks since she'd put her plan into action. You don't realize how much you shut off from the shit until you see a way out. Then, suddenly, the things you've done thoughtlessly for years become awkward, precarious even. Claudette took her clothes off slowly, keeping an eye on Scobie in the mirror. She didn't think too much of stripping in front of him; it was work and common enough. There was a niggle of uneasiness all the same. As Scobie knocked back a few shots of booze she tried to work out what was troubling her. Not the usual nerves, the feeling didn't fit in with them. She looked again at Scobie. Surely he couldn't have found out?

'What time's the punter coming?'

'Nine.'

'Has he got a name?'

'You're to call him James.'

'And where will you be, Scobie, peeping through a hole in the wall?'

It was the wrong thing to say. Scobie jerked his head round to stare at the now naked Claudette. There was a deep frown on his brow and a dark fierceness in his eyes which made Claudette feel scared.

'It was only a crack.'

Scobie didn't reply. He tried to smile but Claudette got the feeling he was hating her for something. She nervously put her hands across herself and cursed silently.

'S-So are you going to give me that gear then?'

For the first time in a long time Scobie was feeling panic. He'd been trying to work out his next move but it just wouldn't come to him. Such a thing hadn't happened before. Most jobs he'd done for the boss had come off naturally. He'd never really needed to think or plan. The Scotch hadn't helped, but it was the other thing, the solid hard-on that really irked him. This sudden manifestation and the urge it provoked seemed far more important than the job he had to do. Scobie felt himself begin to sweat. He frowned even harder and tried to fumble around in his fuzzy brain for a way to go.

'Do you have to stare at me like that?'

'Hello! Are you going to give me the clothes?'

'You want it, don't you, you dirty bastard?'

Scobie went with his senses. Still frowning, he got up from off the bed and put his arms around Claudette. A half-sneer, half-smile flickered across his face and his hands roughly pawed over her.

'Get off me, you fucking shit!'

'Jesus, Claudette . . .'

'Get off!'

Claudette tried to fight Scobie off, but then they both stumbled backwards onto the bed. Scobie forced himself on top, shoved his arm across Claudette's throat and then fumbled for his flies.

'God, I've gotta – Jesus, you are bleedin something.'

'Get off me, you creep! . . . The boss'll kill you! . . . I c-can't bloody well b-breathe!'

Scobie shifted his weight then. He forced himself into Claudette and then pushed both his hands down on her shoulders.

'Bloody hell,' he moaned, 'you are bleedin . . .'

'I'll fucking get you for this, you bastard!'

Claudette tried to struggle against the weight that held

11

her. She tried to spit at the frowning face but her throat was dry. Powerless . . . It was then her sobs began, silent and bitter-tasting.

'Oh . . . Jesus . . . you . . .'

Scobie came. A few feeble, stiff spasms and that was it. Claudette trembled but managed to sneer defiantly at the still frowning face.

'Bastard! Just piss off, will you.'

'Yeh, I will, you stupid little slut. But one thing, right –' Scobie pulled himself forward and put his hands around Claudette's head.

'You're a lousy lay and the fucking boss wants rid of you!'

Scobie sniggered excitedly, then he twisted, right and left, violently, until her neck broke.

2

Last night, saw a face at my window
Sure as hell scared me to death
Thought it was my lover's ghost
Ha – it was only me staring back!

Cymbals danced like bees' wings. The lead guitar wound up a high-pitched scream. Bass and drums thundered as Stevie Kitson bellowed, 'OHHH YEAHH!' and ended the song.

'Oh yeh sure, that's it tonight, brothers and sisters. See you next week – and remember – we love y'all, you Lime Tree people.'

The applause didn't transcend the noise of chat and laughter in the Lime Tree bar. But that was cool because Stevie Kitson and the Slammers didn't do the gig for anything but fun. As Stevie once said, 'Shit, they all talked when Charlie Parker blew his horn. It was the whole scene, man, the music and the vibes.'

Jerry Coton couldn't have agreed more. He'd say, 'You f-fork out a b-bomb to see some group and you're supposed to t-treat them like a snotty soloist in an orchestra. S-Stuff that!' He raised his pint glass and nudged Mary in the arm.

'On form t-tonight.'

'Don't know how he keeps going . . .'

Stevie Kitson was a feature of the local scene, a small-time celebrity. At one time he'd been lead guitar with the Blue Cruisers who had a couple of hits like the famous 'She Ain't What She Is'. He'd made enough out of that to set him up for life, carried on for a while as a session musician, then decided that his hometown and the blues were the place to be.

Jerry lit up a fag and moved his face close to Mary's, enjoying the chance to sneak some intimacy.

'He'll p-probably g-go on till he's grizzled and grey, like us t-too, half dead and t-toothless, still grooving to the same old riffs.'

'You speak for yourself. I'm never growing old . . . I'm going to leave the power on and burn out way before then.'

'I c-could drink to that.'

'Yeh, so could I, cept I haven't got one.' Mary began to ease off her stool. 'You want another?'

'Nah. I'm holding on for V-Vin.'

Thursday nights, the Lime Tree was the place to be. Representatives of all the tribes of the inner city came down. All ages too, groovers and straights, hustlers and tarts. You even got some of the big-time bad guys to shake a finger to good old Stevie, and the odd few cops too, no doubt giving Eileen the landlady the protection to carry on the scene. It was needed. The spliffs were discreet but there to be spotted. The after-hours drinking was regular. It was one of those situations where everything seemed to work without controls. There were no fights or other fuckery. For a few boozy hours, that pub was the melting pot in love. Camaraderie and good vibes transcending the myriad schisms that would normally splinter such a grouping apart. The navvy could boogie with a junkie; the Sikh could spar with Rastafari. Even God made it with the pros, and cops and car thief both agreed Marvin Gaye was supreme. Jerry never wanted such nights to end. Instead of the sour morning-after, he wanted the melting pot to be a magic pot where the party never stopped but grew and grew, bursting out of the walls of the Lime Tree and flooding down every road until the city itself became one huge wild party. He was, of course, well on the way to being stoned.

Outside the pub, you'd have been hard pressed to enjoy yourself. It was bucketing down with rain. Vin St James was locking up his car and cursing the weather, the rain already funnelling down his trilby and onto cold brown hands. He made a dash for the Lime Tree, his last port of call, hoping he'd do good business and make the efforts of the night worthwhile. His foot sloshed into a puddle as he staggered through the doors and into the hall. Vin cursed loudly.

'Don't take it so personal, man. The puddle wasn't put there just for a sucker like you.'

Vin found himself face to face with Scobie Brent. He was leaning against the green tiles in the hall, combing his wet hair. Vin felt a momentary sense of panic at this sudden confrontation and he could only cover his confusion with a lame smile. Then he took off his trilby and tried to coolly flick it down.

'Long time, Scobie,' he said. 'Your kinda weather, huh?'

'You know me, Vin. I take whatever comes, right there.' A smirking Scobie pointed to his chin.

The next move for Vin was to get past Scobie and into the bar without being drawn into some awkward scene. Scobie was a feared heavy and, according to whim, liked to throw his heaviness around. Vin put on one of his best smiles.

'You is one hard case, Scobie,' he said, trying to keep the sarcasm as subtle as possible. 'Didn' me a see you las winter out in the snow wid jus you vest on?'

'The fuck, I was bleedin starkers in the snow!'

15

Vin laughed over loudly and went to push open the bar door.

'So how's your woman doin then, Vin?'

'Eh? Jus fine.' Vin stalled. 'Why you ask? What Claudette to you?'

'Nothin, man, but,' Scobie's smile was mocking, 'you know, I've always kind of fancied her.'

'Oh yeh . . .'

Vin pushed quickly through the bar doors and heaved a sigh of relief. One fuckin mountain a turd! he thought. Inside, the crowd was starting to thin out. Vin ambled through and searched for clients. The half-caste peach with the dishy eyes shook her head. Then he saw nervous Jerry and old grey Frederick. Vin waved. They knew where he'd be.

'D-Didn't think you were g-going to turn up, Vin.'

'Well, Jerry, it a shitty night, me nearly didn' come at all. Me ain't no milkman.'

'More important, man. A weekend smoke is e-ssential.'

'Huh, you shoulda be tuck up in bed, ole man.'

Frederick was somewhere around sixty years old and he never missed a Thursday night. He had a chubby black face that gleamed with sweat, and white frizzed hair. A sharp suit rippled with shine and chunky cufflinks winked gold from his sleeves. Frederick was a groover. Well into ganja, he could score with the girls too. A fine role model, Jerry would think, maybe there's hope after all.

They all sheltered in the entrance to the men's loos as Vin doled out his deals. He was quite a small guy set against the lanky Jerry and Frederick's broad girth. But Vin, though silent, didn't get much aggravation. For first-time customers, he would give off the hard eye, then pull out a slim shiv and groom his nails. That demonstration given, Vin would grin and soothe his clients with the winning sparkle of his eyes. Vin St Charm. It was one way to survive.

'You stayin on feh late drinks, Vin?' Frederick asked.

'Nah man, the ole lady a call.'

'Dem always do but some time you don't have to hear em.'

'Come on, man, it neva pay to be deaf to a woman . . .'

Another latecomer poked his head around the bar door. Des McGinlay, feeling desperate, panic lights in his eyes. He'd been stuck in his house – *loneliness crawling down the walls like so many spiders out to get me*. Des needed company but the boozy energy of the bar made him stall. Smoke and din, sweat on garrulous faces – it seemed to mock him and where he'd fled from. Des groaned, wavered and stared in mild shock at the scene, a scene he should really be part of.

'You gonna kick Winston out? You must be mad!'

'Trust, Bev, it's all about trust, an one thing me do know – only me I trust.'

'Dis horse, it won fuckin hell. Me had fifty soddin quid almost in me hand an den the bastards mek it disqualify!'

'That is cruel . . .'

'You truly are a sweet-looking woman, you know. Why don't we go driving, up to the airport, have a slick supper and watch the planes come in?'

'Promise to take me on one and I just might go . . .'

There wasn't anyone Des could see that he knew. Familiar faces, yes, but no one he could latch onto amid the strident scene. Des knew he shouldn't have come. He'd missed the momentum of the night. The boozy groovers were well off into pleasures shared and Des was just a wet rag, a rain-sodden piece of reality that no one would give two fucks for at that point in time. Des groaned again and then slunk away from the door.

Jerry was still there in the crowd, a smug smile on his face and thoughts of spliffs soon to drift him onto dawn. There was only one thing more he needed that would make it perfect. Jerry scanned the crowd and finally saw her. He began to squeeze his way towards Mary. Yes, it was a bit of a gamble. They were supposed to be just friends but Jerry couldn't help himself, it was the extra buzz he craved. He'd almost reached the bar when he suddenly stopped. Mary was talking to another bloke, a suited geezer with receding black hair and a ponytail, and she was talking in 'that' kind of way, almost drooling over the creep. Jerry's spirits sank. He began to stare vindictively at the git in the suit, seeing there was a finger missing from his left hand. But as he stared, he became conscious of someone else watching him. Jerry turned and found himself looking into a pair of dark, malicious eyes. He shivered like he'd just had a premonition of pain. The eyes narrowed. He saw a deep frown above them and sneering lips below. The tough guy's head nodded towards the door. Jerry was expected to leave. He didn't hesitate. Frustrated and fearful, Jerry walked off and out into the unconsoling rain.

*   *   *

It seemed to be raining everywhere that night. Well beyond the city limits, among the leafy lanes, farmworker Bob Grainger drove home from his local. Fit to burst, he had to stop and take a leak. He pulled in at a lay-by and stumbled over to the bushes. Just as he was about to let go with huge relief, he looked down. The naked corpse of a woman – white skin dripping, eyes puddled with rain – lay right where he was about to piss.

3

Des McGinlay was back in his kitchen and looking out at the rain. A poplar tree shimmered in the breeze; its twisted leaves caught city light and sparkled. Des scowled angrily. He turned on his own light, ignored his gaunt reflection and went to the table to write.

Dear Miranda
    Yeh, it is a mess. And yeh, I'm feeling lousy. But this cold shoulder of yours, it's really screwing me up. What am I supposed to do? You're shagging other guys and I want to shag you . . .

The ball of crumpled paper missed the waste bin. It bounced over lino and hit a wall. The pen bounced too, became silent and blunted on the kitchen floor. Des hugged himself tight. He looked warily at the walls, feeling that the spiders were back again.

'I can't bleedin well take this!'

Grabbing a raincoat, Des again escaped the claustrophobia of his house and hit the streets. He ducked his head into sheets of rain and walked. Up Argent Street, past the Lime Tree and onwards. He trudged twelve miles that night, through the pelting rain, the nameless streets, alone but for half a bottle of whisky. The onslaught of the weather, the pounding his legs received helped to keep at bay those awful questions, that writhing feeling that he was zero and out of control. But the booze was a mistake. The whisky numbed the pain but it sent his mind reeling with unwanted thoughts. Miranda, Miranda, Miranda . . .

The pictures in his mind: smiling eyes, intimate laughter, breasts like speckled pears. He wanted them, wanted to ravish – but someone else would be there. Des groaned up at the streetlights, stashed his empty bottle in a hedge, crawled on through the rain-drenched night.

*   *   *

'Where is he then?'
  'Fuck knows.'
'It's gone twelve o'clock.'
'I know, he ain't been himself lately.'
'What, he's still moping over that bird of his?'
'Yeh, like a lost dog looking for its master.'
'A wanker if you ask me.'
'The cops want to speak to him now.'
'Jesus, what's that about, Wayne?'
'Fuck knows.'
The Fedora used to be called the Black Boy. No one was quite sure what the old name referred to. Some swarthy king from the past? The times when aristocrats paraded their houseboy Negroes around? Or a reference to those Victorian urchins shoved up chimneys or pushed down mines? Whatever, in modern times, Black Boy was no name a brewery would wish to be saddled with. But Fedora, that had glamour; it was Hollywood stars and cool dudes in the gleaming city.

Midday, Des McGinlay looked through the pub window and saw the grainy black and white blow-ups of famous faces. But no one sat by the parlour palms. No smoke drifted to the ceiling fans. There were no heavy-drinking role-players on the New Orleans scene. Des sighed as he pushed through the doors.

Wayne was slotting pint mugs on a rack above the bar. He didn't look at Des when he entered. Dick O'Malley sat on a bar stool and grinned. The ever-present, ever-grinning Dick nodded at Des and then gormlessly stared into his beer.

'Sorry I'm late.'

There was no immediate response. Wayne carried on stacking glasses and his grizzled chin gave nothing away. Finally, however, the words came.

'You look really bad, Des. Terminal. You look like you got TB, cancer and Aids all in one go.'

'There's a hangover for you.'

'You've got to pull yourself together, mate.' Wayne brought his hairy forearms down to the bar and gave Des a sad look. 'You know I don't mind a bit of slack, but this ain't no sheltered home for the fucked up.'

'I know.'

'I mean, there's gotta be some point to me being boss, like I can put my feet up and give you the run around.'

Des had been working at the Fedora for six months. It was temporary, of course, until his other job picked up. But the whole set-up there was a temporary affair. The Fedora was the kind of city centre pub which had a different clientele every day (grinning Dick was an exception). It went through bar staff on a monthly basis and even Wayne had no inclinations to stay around. The Fedora was a kind of floating world, an on-the-off-chance place that meant nothing to no one.

'Maybe you should take the rest of the week off?' Wayne was now picking his teeth with a match. 'That new bird Kim was asking for a few extra hours.'

'I don't know, Wayne. It might be better if I came in.'

'Come on, you ain't that desperate. A break'd probably do you good.'

Wayne had a thing about matches. He cleaned his nails, teeth and even his ears with them. He scraped them on his bristled chin, passed them through his fingers and made pretty patterns on the bar.

'I don't know what I'd do, though. You know, things are still slack.'

'Anyways, you're wanted. The police are asking for you.'

'Oh no . . .'

'Don't ask me why. You do anything stupid lately?'

'Don't think so.'

'Better to keep yourself scarce.' Wayne proceeded to slot some matches into his fist. 'And that client of yours, posh Rebecca, she rang up, wants to know how you're getting on.'

Des found it hard to focus on the idea that he was wanted, even if by the police. A world-weary sigh hissed out of him.

'Come on, Des, the whole boring load of crap will still be here when you get back.' Wayne raised his fist. Suddenly he scraped the match heads against his stubble. There was laughter all round when his hand became fire.

*　　*　　*

Lunchtime was a gaping hole, an empty stomach, a great white craving for a fag. Jerry Coton, having spent hours climbing out of sleep, finally climbed out of bed. He threw on his dressing gown and shuffled to the fire-escape door. 'Shit,' he moaned, 'save me from oblivion.' Pushing the door open, he saw red roofs and rain-washed leaves. His bleary eyes tried to focus and his whole body wavered, almost shrank from the painful glare. Jerry lit a cigarette and waited for the view to sink in, for the world to stop being upside down. Once adjusted, he moved onto the top step and looked out. 'Another aimless d-day in the sprawl, another stroll on the streets of d-deferred opportunity,' he muttered, half smiling to himself. But it wasn't a comfortable smile. Dope smugness worked up to a point, but anxiety always lurked somewhere. Jerry thought then that he saw the houses shift as though they were floating on water and he was relieved when he heard noises coming from the kitchen below. Gripping the shaky banister hard, Jerry sighed and went on down. Mary was there, starting to wash up. She offered to make him toast. Jerry gave the door some support and tried not to leer.

'So, Jerry, you want to know what happened?'

Since waking, in the back of his mind Jerry had been wondering and hoping that last night had been a flop for Mary. Now she was looking at him as friend and confidant and he was forced to brace himself.

'You know, with that guy last night?'

'Oh, yeh . . . the one with the f-finger m-missing.'

'Weird and a turn-on. I know he did look a bit slimy but we kind of hit it off.'

Jerry clamped his lips together and tried to look unmoved.

'His name was Ross, said he sold cars.' Mary grimaced. '*That* was a turn-off.'

'S-So what h-happened?'

'You know. I mean, why am I telling you?'

'The g-geezer stayed the n-night?'

Jerry's heart plummeted and squirmed with jealousy. He struggled to hide it.

'See what you miss when you get up late?'

'S-So,' Jerry managed to gulp, 'h-how, how was it?'

'Interesting. You should've heard what he said about his finger.'

'I – I c-can imagine.'

'But it wasn't that good. To tell the truth, at the end of it, he seemed more interested in my darkroom than me, and kept asking if I took dirty pictures.'

'You said he looked s-slimy.' Jerry began to feel relieved.

'Yeh, one down to experience I reckon.'

Mary went back to washing up while Jerry struggled to settle his feelings. *Ponytailed little ponce! Slime bag!* But then he remembered the eyes, the cold little eyes that had sent him running and he shivered. *Mary, those careless risks she took . . .*

*   *   *

It was all laid out there in front of him. A pile of beer cans on the living-room floor, overflowing ashtrays and a few roaches stubbed out in a plant pot. The kitchen told the same story, only this time a bottle of Scotch lorded it above the crumpled balls of paper on the floor. Des stood in the doorway and could feel the pull. The 'big wallow' that grinned and whispered seductively, *Come on, man, sit down and let's binge.* He did his best at self-control, grabbed a bin bag and flung the mess of the night's turmoil into it. Outside, the garbage got squashed satisfyingly into an already full bin. Cautiously, Des breathed in cool air, wondering whether this could be his fresh start. He wiped rain off a plastic chair, sat down and got out the local newspaper.

The headline on the front page was briefly intriguing. The body of a naked woman, possibly a prostitute, had been found in a lay-by five miles outside the city. Reference was made to the fact that several others had been found in similar circumstances over the past two years. Des was interested in that. One of the bodies previously found was that of a whore who'd lived just down the road and at the time he'd put out feelers to see if it could bring him some work. This woman had had no friends or adult relatives, though. Just a five-year-old girl left in the worst of lurches. Des sighed; he was in the wrong neighbourhood, close to the wrong clientele. He threw the newspaper down. The patio seemed dismal and empty. He stared at the grime on the paving stones and took a wary look at an insipid sky.

The colour caught his eye first. A hint of red amid the dreary backs of the houses. Des turned his head and saw it properly. A red balloon was bouncing down from his roof. Slowly it drifted and, catching a current of air from the entry, it suddenly flung itself forwards and landed at Des's feet. Des smiled slightly at the surprise, but then felt a stab of resentment at the intrusion and kicked out. A square of polythene was attached to the balloon. Des picked it up. On one side of the square he read: *Open me. I want to be let out! Please!!!!!*

Des carefully unstuck the sellotape at the side and drew out a pink card. More writing: *From the mystry? Who loves you and is ready for it – sex. This is from Lisa. I love you. I live at 108 Kingsvale Tower.*

Des stared at the message. He looked back up at the blanket of clouds. It was then that the ache began to return, that thwarted hunger as chillingly tangible as the need for food.

It took some time to find the *A–Z*, such was the mess of his house. He began to flick through the pages. He must've been up that way when he was taxi-driving. But that was then, when he was with Miranda. Now the lines and letters were just a blur. The map book to the city had a random index and false reference codes. But Kingsvale Tower did exist. The name finally pointed itself out of the confusion and Des realized that a westerly wind must have brought the balloon two miles through the polluted air. He pondered. Was this luck or just a hoax from a silly girl? Could it be a real message from a lusting damsel locked up high in a tower? Could this be his escape from the claws that dug into him? Des closed the *A–Z*, put it in his back pocket and went to the phone.

'Is Rebecca there, please?'

'Sorry, she hasn't been in work for a couple of days.'

Des smiled with relief. 'Could you tell her Mr McGinlay rang, yeh?'

'Certainly.'

Des grabbed his coat and hurried to the front door. As he opened it, two burly policemen stopped and stared at him. One had a scar that halved his nose.

4

The cop with the scar-spliced nose leaned over towards Des and snarled. You could tell he'd had his fair share of abuse about his deformity and toughed it out. In fact, he wore it with pride.

'Look, when Miranda said "shove it", she didn't mean shove a house brick through the windscreen of her car!'

'But, I didn't . . . I don't –'

'Were you out last night?'

'In most of the time though I did go for a bit of a walk.'

'Pissed, were you?'

'I suppose I was a –'

'Stoned?'

'You don't expect me to –'

'Yeh, too bloody high to know it. Too red with rage to care.'

'Come on, she lives six miles from me. You think I'd walk there and back, twelve miles in the pouring rain, just to smash a car window?'

'She's a tasty bird, Miranda. You must be pretty sick at losing her.'

'And smashing her car will help me get her back?'

'It was a cry from the heart, attention-seeking; and you got it too. Miranda clocked you, mate.'

'Oh, I don't know, maybe I did do it. But if I did, it was a mistake. I was pissed and –'

'That's no defence.'

'Oh sod it, man. Miranda won't press charges anyway.'

The cop ceased to flaunt his disfigurement. He eased back in his chair and allowed an indulgent smile to soften his mean interrogator's face.

'Well, if you did do it, and Miranda does press charges, then you're in deep shit, aren't you?'

'What you mean?'

'This Mickey Mouse licence of yours, "private investigator". Business good, is it?'

'Fair enough.'

'Oh yeh? Well, mate, your days of snooping on unfaithful wives could be over. Mickey Mouses ain't supposed to have criminal records.'

'Ha bloody ha.'

'So, we'd better get the charge sheet filled out, and a statement written down.'

*   *   *

There comes a time, in the stages of splitting up, when lost love becomes hate. When all those yearning touchstones of desire are turned on their head and become foul urges to destroy. As he walked out of the police station, Des got a sense of that, like a sudden spurt of acid through his veins. But, valiantly, he clung to hope and dived for the first phone box he found.

'Is Miranda there, please?'

'It is me.'

'Yeh? Well this is Des, I've just got out of the cop shop!'

'You mean they haven't locked you up?'

'Come on, Miranda. I was pissed and angry.'

'I don't want you harassing me. I don't want you anywhere near me!'

'Look, I'll pay for the windscreen and everything.'

28

'I don't want this phone call, Des.'

'You're not really going to press charges, are you?'

'Oh yes I bloody well am! I'd press for the death penalty if I had the chance, anything to get you out of my hair.'

'Jesus, you don't have to be such a shit. I could lose my PI licence and be stuck down the Fedora for the rest of my life.'

'Look, Des, I'm sorry, but it is over, and your day in court will hopefully make it plain to you that it is finally and totally finished. So please, just get off the phone and get on with your own life.'

Des stared at the silent mouthpiece and the streaks of grime around its rim. He sensed something within him that was becoming familiar. A draining away inside, a feeling that the ground beneath his feet was turning liquid.

'I've got to do something!'

Des dashed up the road, clambered into his rusty old Lancia and sped off.

He knew where he was going but didn't want to admit it to himself. Instead, he began to wonder whether he would lose his licence and whether or not it was worth having anyway. Business was barely ticking over. He hadn't actually been properly paid since he'd sorted out Calvin Westmoreland, the guy with the gammy leg who'd ripped off Sister Bethany's savings. True, he did have a case on the go, if only he could get round to working on it.

'I'm sure my husband is having an affair, Mr McGinlay, and I just need the proof. And if he is, I'm going to get a divorce. I'm going to bleed the rotten bugger dry!'

Fine. Posh Rebecca had the means and Des was keen to provide the ammunition. But Rebecca's prospective ex proved to be slippery as well as rotten and Des had yet to get conclusive proof.

'What am I paying you for, Mr McGinlay?'

'I'm sorry, but your husband plans his shagging like he's a frigging spook in the Kremlin.'

'You have two weeks or I go elsewhere!'

'I'll do it,' Des grumbled to himself. 'Miranda may have stabbed me in the back and left me writhing, but I'll bleeding well do it.'

That was a week ago and Des had barely been sober since.

*   *   *

Night was falling fast around the Kings Road Estate. Already towerblocks were dark monoliths, and menacing stars were piercing the clear sky. Des shivered in the exposed grass spaces he roamed across. The towers, as their lights came on, began to seem almost homely. Kingswood, Kingsriver, Kingsacre (renamed Kingsarse by some local hood) and then, finally, Kingsvale. Des clutched his little pink card and looked up. No desperate face at the window, no balloon escaping to the stars, but Des chose to remain optimistic and blind.

Empty corridors and landings. Resolutely closed doors. There's something ferociously hostile about a towerblock, as though when entering you defile the dead or taunt their living, ghostly spirits. Des had always hated towerblock calls when he drove his taxi. Standing on a cold landing late at night, hearing dogs growl, feeling eyes at spyholes, screams and laughter echoing down the pipes. He almost chickened out as the lift shuddered open at Kingsvale Tower, but he doggedly took the plunge. Maybe it was a stupid waste of time or maybe a sniff of adventure, but it was something that took him away from *her*. Des stood outside number 108, took a deep breath and rang the bell.

She could've been sixteen, Des thought, perhaps even seventeen. It was hard to tell, the way young girls bloom. She could've been twelve.

'Yes? What d'you want?'

'Hi there. Your name Lisa?'

'Who's askin?'

Whatever her age, the young lady had all the components of a perfectly formed body; and she'd made the effort to let the world know this by wearing a dress that clung to her like a coating of smooth, erotic moss.

'Well, hope you don't mind but . . .'

'Yes?'

Lisa – this girl was surely her – was beginning to retreat from the door. She had a pretty face but her lips were sulky and there was hardness in her eyes.

'I reckoned it was a good idea, this card. Literally out of the blue. Risky, yes. Crazy, but . . . you know, nice. Like the lottery, seeing what comes up – me.' Des tried a charm smile but he was fast realizing that perhaps Lisa didn't quite appreciate him turning up. He suddenly noticed a picture of a blue Madonna hanging like a warning sign in the hallway.

'Oh my God! Jesus! Look, you just get –'

'The name's Des – I was wondering, why don't we throw caution to the winds and meet up some time?'

'It was a joke, you daft –'

As Lisa began to hiss and close the door, Des saw a man's face peer into the hall. A father's face, no doubt, large and stern-looking.

'What's going on, Lisa? Who is that?'

'Dunno, Dad,' Lisa called back and then turned to Des. 'Just piss off, will you?'

'You don't reckon, huh?'

'It's not one of your boyfriends sniffing around, is it?'

'No, Dad, it's some stranger. But – he's talking dirty, Dad, bout me.'

'What?'

Des caught her malicious little smile before the extent of his own stupidity hit him like a punch in the gut. Seeing a burly father come down the hall towards him, he backed away, looking for a hole to jump into.

'Let me see this bloke.'

'I – I think he's a bit funny, Dad.'

Des took one more step back, hit a wall and then realized that the only honourable thing to do was run. The door to 108 was flung open as Des frantically rushed to the stairs.

'Is that the bleeder?'

'Yeh, I think he's one of them perverts.'

'Eh, you, come here!'

Des pushed through the stairwell doors, footsteps pounding behind him. The rest was madness. Zigzagging pell-mell down ten sets of stairs. His steps echoing, and heavier, more menacing footsteps close behind. And then the shouts, the raucous shouts that seemed to fill the whole tower, bringing blunt shafts of embarrassment to Des's ears.

'Just let me get you! . . . Fuckin perverts should be trashed! . . . Gonna beat the livin shits outa you! . . . Bastaaard!!'

*   *   *

Vin St James sat down beside a clump of rosebay willowherb and thought about being a suspect for murder. He felt calm enough. He hadn't done the deed but he knew that didn't count for much if a sucker was needed. Vin knew he was sitting pretty for that, a dumb-arse black pimp would do fine if the real killer couldn't be found. There was a lot to think about and the patch of wasteground wedged between two canals and a factory yard was the only place he could go to think. It was his place and the ganja plants that gracefully swayed in the darkness were his winter supply. Vin took out his knife and stabbed at the ground.

Me gotta tink it out firs, den feel. Shit, Claudette! It coulda bin some friggin white nut, some half-dere shit who took she away. Bad feh me, dem don't often catch such creeps who melt away like snow in the bloodclaat suburbs.

32

But she wasn' s'pose fi be out on the game. Wha she a say?
Gwan see a fren? Jesus, what was the bleedin bitch a doin?

Vin dropped his knife and let his hands hang against his thighs. He sighed loudly, thinking how the cops knew he wasn't the one but were laughing at his predicament: A drink down the Earl eh, St James, one in the Vine and the Lime Tree, you shouldn't have to worry bout witnesses then, pal, you should be cast iron in the clear. But then maybe they'll have bad memories about knowing a piece of shit like you?

So plan one was obvious to Vin; he had to get some guys to back him up. But what if it wasn't a nutter? What if Claudette had done something stupid and got caught up in bad business? She was pissed off enough to make that possible. Vin came face to face with his feelings then. *Shit, me ain't no pimp. We was partners, a team, man, seeking good returns an a straight way out. Jesus, me fuckin love her an me heart it bleed!*

Vin knew what his second plan had to be. He'd have to start asking around, check out the other players on the scene and seek an explanation. It was dangerous but he had to know if Claudette had been messing him around. In the distance he heard trains trundling into the mainline station and above the tops of the weeds he saw the lights of city centre towers muted in grey haze. He stabbed his blade back into the wet earth and tried not to think about regret and his really big mistake.

Jesus, man, it happen. What the diff'rence, it all come out the same . . .

*   *   *

Driving the Lancia through sparkling city streets was soothing. Des felt the shakes recede and his heartbeat ease down to its normal level. It had been a close shave. Lisa's angry father had tripped over, giving Des the chance to sneak off into the night. Now, feeling quite cosy amid the anonymous suburbs, he allowed himself a smile and a little self-scolding too. *What a stupid dickhead! Total prat! Look what it's doing to me, Miranda.* A mistake to think that one. The name Miranda, it was a trigger; it was like a bell to a conditioned dog. Des didn't actually salivate, but physiological ructions did occur. Most of all, he suddenly began to feel that awful hunger, that dreadful appetite for release. He almost howled then because his search for Lisa, no matter how stupid, had given him a goal, had put his craving on the outside. Now he was back to the prospect of a lonely house, the big wallow with its bad vibes and alcoholic stupor. Des gripped the steering wheel hard. *I've got to do something!*

It was then that a sort of solution did arise. He'd just turned into a side street when he came to a group of Asian men standing on the pavement. Des blinked. They were carrying placards. He slowed down and peered through his windscreen. KEEP KERB-CRAWLERS OUT! NO GO FOR PROS! Des realized he was coming up to Burma Road, well known for its streetwalkers and inviting window displays. An idea began to illuminate his mind but before it could grow, an Asian guy tapped on his window. Des wound it down.

'Hope you don't mind me askin, mate, but what're you doin round here?'

'Reckon I do mind.'

'You're not local, are you?'

'It's just none of your business, friend.'

'We think it is, mate. We're sick of kerb-crawlers and dirty pros fuckin up the lives of our women and kids and we're out to stop them. So, are you looking for sex or what?'

'Come off it, man. I don't mind you demonstrating but what I do is my business and I'm not bleeding well telling you'

'Oh yeh?'

'Yeh.'

'Right, we're gonna take your number, right, and we're gonna give it to the police and we're gonna tell them what a dirty fucker you are.'

'Too late, they already know.'

Des pressed down the accelerator and moved off from the group. A couple of them briefly ran after him, shouting abuse. On the corner of Burma Road a group of elderly Asian men sat on milk crates. They brandished their fists at Des. He waved back and slowly turned into the famous road. It was deserted. No bare thighs flashed out between the trees. No bosoms pressed against parlour windows. That faint spark of an idea in Des's mind began to wane.

But it didn't die. Des cruised down Burma Road and then on through the backstreets. Barely half a mile from the vigilantes, his headlights caught a familiar sight. Des slowed. Should he try? He never had before. Never needed to. But wasn't that what they were for? When you were down on your luck, when there was no one else to turn to? Des stopped next to the woman and she peered in through the open window.

'Bad time for business,' he muttered.

'Could say that.'

'You're brave to be out here.'

'You've got to make a living whatever.'

'Guess so . . . erm, what do you charge then?'

'What d'you want?'

'Intercourse I guess.'

'That's thirty.'

'OK.'

'I've got a room across the way.'

She said her name was Pearl, and a pearl she was, a yellow pearl, slightly oriental in looks and with bright ginger hair.

35

Des followed her ample backside up the narrow stairs of a dingy house. A smell of damp caught his nostrils, a whiff of ganja and air freshener too. They entered a small bedroom on the first floor, an empty dismal place with just a bed, table and easy chair. Des began to waver. This was another nothing place, a functional fuck-room that made him feel depressed. The feeling was made worse by the token picture on the wall. A mournful clown with a big grin looked over at him. Pearl quickly put down her bag, laid a condom on the bedside table and then began to strip. It didn't take her long. A miniskirt and top and that was it, apart from her calf-length boots, which she left on. She lay down on the bed and smiled while Des stood hovering awkwardly in the middle of the room. She was, he could see, a perfect erotic vision, the sort of vision that was meant to provoke wild love-making, but –

'Are you OK, luv?' she said.

'Dunno yet.'

But Des knew what had happened. He'd messed up again. In his mind, yes, she was erotic perfection, but there on the bed, she might just as well have been a pile of flesh with a scar.

'Would you like me to come over and undress you, help you get started?'

'Look, Pearl, I . . .'

He couldn't really pretend she was Miranda, they were too different. Anyway, such fantasies rarely worked, and wouldn't in a place so perfunctory. He looked again at the sentimental clown and wanted to mash its face. Time was what he needed to get involved with Pearl's body, to make it fit the contours of his own desire, but there wasn't time on the game. She must've read his thoughts.

'Are you going to do it or what? I haven't got all night.'

'Pearl, you are great but . . . I don't think this is going to work, I'm sorry.'

'After coming this far you don't want to?'

'Well, I guess I do, but . . .'

'Bloody hell, what are you? A peeping tom or something? Jesus!'

Pearl angrily got up off the bed and began to put her clothes back on.

'If things aren't bad enough with these vigilantes, I have to land myself with a limp john! Fuck –'

'I'll pay you some money anyway.'

'You bet you will.'

'A tenner?'

'It'll do. Now, come on, out.' Pearl smoothed over the bed and picked up her handbag. 'Jesus, this city is full of wankers . . . religious nuts . . . murdering perverts.'

'You knew the woman who got killed?'

'Yeh, I knew her, thought she had more sense.'

'The risks you take, though, Pearl.'

'Part of the game, just like prats like you.'

'No hard feelings I hope.'

'Nah, you're all right. I got part of my fee, but get out now, huh.'

Pearl opened the door. 'What you need, sweetheart, is a nice girlfriend, right?'

She winked as Des passed her and then drifted on down the dingy stairway. He was trying to think of a journey, a different journey that didn't cruise through familiar streets and end up at the same old bottle.

5

Posh Rebecca's husband was called Theo. He was a university lecturer, some kind of expert on the history of sanitation. Des could see why Rebecca wanted rid of him. Theo was small and flabby. He sported a brown moustache. He had dandruff. The moustache was no doubt the sign of his eccentric trade, for otherwise Theo looked like a bland executive, stepping out sprightly in expensive suits with a sly look to his eye. Des blended in well on the campus, got a fix on him easily enough. Theo had a fancy woman all right. Naomi; a skinny, hawk-nosed lady almost half his age. Des clocked the little glances, the hand-holds beneath tables and the secret sniggers. But that was the easy part. Catching Theo on an assignation proved much harder. Twice he'd tailed him on unscheduled drives and twice he'd lost him. But this time Des was ready, he hoped.

He sat in his car outside the campus entrance on the afternoon when Theo usually went screwing. For a lovelorn, doped-up fool, Des felt quite reasonable. He'd indulged the night before, but something had shifted within him and he didn't feel as though he was treading water so much any more. That he put down to his stupidity. Making an ass of himself, it seemed, was something he had to do. But it was perhaps due also to another kind of resolution, the late-night kind. What do washed-out guys do? Concentrate on work. So there he was, businesslike, out on the streets and doing his job. He looked with a pin-sharp eye at the campus scene and scanned for a red BMW. With effort, the M word was kept from his thoughts. He did wonder though about a possible court case. Did he really sling a brick at her car? This was a tricky problem. No way he could reason with – the accuser. One possibility came to him: a consultation with his only friend in the police force. There must be ways to sort out such things, and Errol would know them. Thus preoccupied, Des almost missed the red BMW, but recovered in time to get on its tail.

It was going to be the same switch. Theo parked in Sainsbury's car park, got out and went into the store. Des had worked out what would happen next. Theo would go left into the store café, exit through a side door and then slip through to the DIY warehouse on the same site. He would go in and out again and meet up with Naomi on its parking lot. Des drove round to the relevant entrance and waited. Across the vast area of cars, he soon spotted the portly figure with the trim moustache. Through his binoculars he saw the glint in the eye and the jokey, surreptitious manoeuvres Theo made as though it was a jolly good game. A blue Ford Fiesta exited the car park and Des followed his unwary prey home.

Naomi and Theo parked in the drive of a house at the end of a modern terrace. There was a low fence around the house and plenty of greenery. As the couple went inside, Des found himself stalling. How was he going to get any decent shots? Did he really want to scrabble around in the undergrowth and snoop? Wasn't it, after all, just plain sex? Des almost convinced himself. Then a piercing view of the big wallow came to him and he wrenched open the car door. A few minutes later he was shuffling through a big rhododendron at the back of Naomi's garden. Luck was with him. Naomi had a large picture window. She also had the courtesy to snog Theo right in the middle of Des's lens.

'That ought to satisfy Rebecca,' he muttered. 'Specially as Theo's got his hand crawling up Naomi's thigh. God, whatever, wouldn't mind my hand . . .'

Des brought the camera down. This is getting too close. What if Rebecca wants the full gory details? How would I cope? he asked himself.

Des looked at the upstairs of the house and began to wonder how seasoned pros get such shots. He couldn't see any way short of a ladder to do it. But luck was still with him. The two lovers had begun undressing each other in the living room. They were having quite a giggle and Naomi feigned great shock when she saw Theo unveil his upright tool. Then a game of 'catch-me' began and the two ran off naked, both laughing like little kids. Des took what pictures he could, his fingers shaky and sweat on his brow.

'Shit,' Des breathed as he replaced the lens cap. 'That was too close. What do you get when you make a move? Your own bleeding needs thrown back at you. Unwanted fuckery I say, like so many memories left stale in the mouth the morning after, too damn much.'

*   *   *

'Des still not in then, eh?'
   'Nah, he took the full week off.'
   'Can't see him lasting much longer.'
   'Des's all right. I mean, let's face it, Dick, it's a crap job.'
   'His other option seems pretty weird.'
   'Well, he's still getting the phone calls.'
   'But does he get the dough, eh, Wayne?'
   'Fuck knows. But who gives a shit, let him do it.'
   'So where's this bird then who's doing his shift?'
   'In later, and pretty dishy too I tell you.'
   'Ten times better than Des.'
   'Phew, no comparison.'

'So what you reckon your chances are?'

'Fuck knows.'

Des managed to enter the Fedora with a certain amount of style. He caught the gaze of Bogart on the wall and thought, Yeh, well, it's only acting after all. Match in mouth, Wayne straightened up and raised an eyebrow.

'Give us a malt, and one for yourself,' Des said as he plonked his camera on the bar. 'I reckon I've earned some dosh today.'

'Well, Jesus, this is a major happening, Des.'

'See the morgue's still empty, apart from Dick that is.'

'Ha, ha.'

'So what you done then, solved the perfect crime?' Wayne flicked his match up into the air with his lips and got it into the ice bucket.

'No, just done my bit for the divorce rate.'

'That ain't hard to do these days.'

'Got some snaps up at the lab now. I'll have them in an hour.'

'Dirty sod. Still, you're looking half normal, Des, and that's a big improvement. If you got that bleeding Miranda out of your hair, well, Jesus, I wouldn't know you.'

'Don't mention her.'

'I mean,' Dick said, trying to get in on the conversation, 'what did happen with you and that bird?'

'Don't – mention – her!'

Des leaned over towards Dick and fixed him with a hard stare. The work he'd done may have been troublesome but it had helped; an aspirin for the heart, and he didn't need a meddling prat to ruin its effect.

'Forget it,' Wayne intervened. 'A bust-up's a bust-up, ain't it, Des? Nothing else to it.'

'Yeh, full stop to that.' Des turned his attention back to his whisky. 'So, Wayne, any messages for me?'

'As it happens, yeh. This woman, Bertha, she wants to see you, said it was "very serious business".'

*   *   *

Someone was having difficulty crossing the road. He was hovering hesitantly on the kerbside and looking extremely worried. But this was no inexperienced child, or an elderly guy fearful his creaky legs wouldn't make the crossing. This was Jerry Coton and he was stoned. 'What the hell was in that j-joint?' he was muttering. 'The whole w-world looks set to explode!'

Jerry had been out for the afternoon to see a dole friend. A pleasant activity with shared joints and gallons of coffee. There was the usual half-cocked homespun philosophy and obsessive concentrations on the rhythms of rock. 'Shi-it, that bass line, it really moved!' But on leaving for home, Jerry felt like he'd walked out into a nightmare. The trees on the streets suddenly seemed alive, with tiny eyes and limbs groping. People's faces too seemed odd: luminescent and caricatured. As he reached the shops on the main road, a large crate of oranges on the pavement flared up like a brazier of fire. Jerry's thoughts then were only of home, until he went to cross the road.

'They're all g-going too b-bloody fast! Well, they look slow in the d-distance but, Jesus, when they c-come up to you –'

Jerry felt he had to talk out his thoughts just to give them some sense of reality.

'That's the b-bleedin d-drivers, though, isn't it? They do that, ease d-down hoping you'll take the p-plunge and then accelerate j-just to give you a scare.'

He looked round. There were some traffic lights a short way up the road but the thought of crossing at that point made him just as nervous.

'Walking out in front of revving c-cars, their eyes and feet primed for amber, then someone t-turning into the m-main road and smashing you down. No way.'

Jerry hugged himself and shuddered. He could ask someone for help but, either way, they or him would come over weird. He looked back into the road.

'Jesus, the t-tarmac, what if I went to cross and s-sank straight through?'

*   *   *

Des McGinlay sat in Daley's wine bar and felt the tension in his shoulders. Outside, expressway traffic streaked the night with red and amber. He looked at the streams of light – *could be transient firebugs flitting through tall tower moulds of ants. It's a jungle out there after all*. Des shuddered and turned his attention to the gleaming pool of whisky that sat before him. He studied its golden glow. He could almost breathe it in and he felt an acute sense of temptation. It would be easy to drift slack, drown in sorrow and blame 'M'. *A sweet fix of poison and a healthy 'sod you' . . . a working philosophy well enough*. Des smiled but then saw the envelope of photos on the table in front of him. Now there was bitter crap. Joy, deceit and betrayal packaged 10 x 8 and barely a centimetre thick. Were they worth more than a boozy oblivion? Des didn't get a chance to answer himself. Rebecca suddenly sat down before him.

Rebecca, forty years old, putting on weight with butcher's cheeks and pale grey hair, seemed nervous. She flustered about with her purse, couldn't decide whether to get a drink and looked cagily all around her. Despite her earlier forthrightness, Des could see that this was a big moment for Rebecca. Her only marriage, maybe her only partner, she had subscribed to and believed in the Great White

Wedding. Now some seedy, on-the-make jerk was going to prise her life apart. Bitter crap indeed.

'S-So, I suppose you've found out?'

'Do you really want to know? I mean, we can forget all this.'

'I – I –'

'Just a bit of folly. Believe me, I know. Even at forty, people do some really stupid things and the only thing you can do is forget them. I mean, I've got a bad memory, and my bill – well, you can just write it off as a mistake.'

Rebecca sat and stared at Des for quite a while after that. It was somewhat disconcerting. Her head held erect and haughty but her lips and chin were quivering, seemingly about to dissolve.

'You want a drink?'

'N-No . . . no, I'm all right. I was just thinking about what you said.'

'As I said, whatever you want to do.'

'This is an important moment for me.'

'I know. It's easy to set up an investigation in anger, but it's much harder when the results come in.'

'You're not that insensitive, are you? You seem almost decent.'

'No more messed up than most.'

'I suppose I could forget it and try to ignore everything that goes on behind my back.'

'Oh yeh, you could. You don't have to talk to me about easy options.'

'But I have to know really, otherwise . . .'

'Yeh, I guess you wouldn't want to live with a lie.'

'So?'

'The answer, as you've probably guessed, is yes. The woman is a research assistant called Naomi Kent. They have it off a few afternoons a week at her place. It's all there in the photos, but you may not want to look.

Thinking of divorce proceedings though, well, you've got the shit where you want him.'

Rebecca put her hand on the envelope and tentatively tapped her fingers. Des thought her chin was really going to drop off.

'God, I feel awful,' she said.

'Let me get you a drink.'

'I don't think I do want to see the photos yet.'

'It can help to get pissed, you know. Makes you think about revenge, helps you murder him in your mind. It's a way of trying to break free. I've been working on it myself for months now, all that frigging pain you've got to shift . . .'

But Rebecca wasn't listening. Her eyes went off to the flow of the traffic, the tall towers where people were ants and the city was a big, lonely place.

*   *   *

As soon as he opened the door, Des knew he was in for a hard time. Brown eyes, upfront and probing, hit his own and he almost stepped backwards. Previously, he'd been eyeing up a bottle of Scotch and wondering whether he deserved some celebration. But Des couldn't quite give himself permission. His motives for indulging seemed doubtful. That woman again. It had been stalemate until the doorbell rang.

'You Des McGinlay then?'

'Sure am.'

'Glad I've found you. I'm Bertha Turton.' Bertha looked around in a doubtful manner. 'Thought you blokes had offices above laundrettes and the like, not pub landlords taking messages.'

'I'm working on it,' Des replied. 'But you found me anyway.'

Des invited Bertha in. He switched on the light in his

front room and sat her down on an old easy chair. She still seemed doubtful, looking at the bare table, battered filing cabinet and sofa that filled out the rest of the room.

'Yeh, this is my office,' Des said, 'until I get the cash together for a proper place. This, and the Fedora, which is where I kind of entertain clients.'

'S'pose you have to start somewhere.'

Bertha Turton was a tall woman. Somewhere in her mid-forties, she had a pale, attractive face, but looked pinched and drawn. Her neglected bleached hair was like grass the winter had killed. She stretched out her long legs and Des reminded himself to focus on work.

'I've heard about you. You used to go out with Ceceline, right, but then got hooked up with a bitch called Miranda and disappeared off the scene.'

'How the hell you know that?'

'Just a bit of asking around. People don't take you too seriously as a private investigator. Just someone else spinning a line, but they reckon your heart's in the right place. They say you know how to handle yourself.'

'Great. So why have you bothered coming?'

'Because you are known. Because maybe I can keep an eye on you and trust you to stay on my side.'

'The client is all with me, but, you know, money. The reason I don't have much of a track record is because the people who come to me don't have any. I've just wrapped up a job though.'

Bertha's eyes probed again and Des shifted in his seat. She smiled quietly to herself.

'Whatever the rates, I have the money.'

'Ah, so what's the job?'

'The biggest thing you've ever snooped into.'

Prostitutes have mothers. That was the thing that lit her anger and fuelled her pride. Some dirty whore ends up dead in a lay-by. Who cares? The mother does. Bertha didn't flinch as she told Des about the death of her daughter Claudette. The phone call from the police, the trip to the morgue, and the forensic details of her death.

'It was hard, very hard; and the police were hard too, as though a prostitute's mother didn't count for so much.'

'I read about it in the paper. I'm sorry, Bertha, I really, I mean I don't know –'

Des was shocked. He didn't think he'd end up with this kind of offer of work. Missing persons, adultery – fine; but murder? Bertha seemed to sense this.

'Look, you know the police aren't going to put much energy into this, and won't get far anyway because who's going to talk to them?'

'Yeh, but this is deep water.'

Bertha pulled out a handkerchief and blew her nose. No tears. She was resolutely, almost vindictively, calm.

'But Claudette wasn't supposed to be out on the game that night. If she was, Vin would've been round to protect her.'

'You mean it could've been local, someone she knew?'

'Someone I know! If it was, Des, I want that arsehole and I want him nailed.'

'Have you got any other reasons to suspect . . . ?'

'Yeh, she left me a parcel to look after. I opened it the other day; it had over five thousand quid in it!'

Bertha Turton gave Des a defiant look, her brown eyes once again piercing straight into those that were blue.

The money, was it really the money that made Des suddenly get keen? He shifted in his seat, uncomfortable that he might so easily be bought, so easily tempted into a dangerous situation. Or was it Bertha's sudden smile? Intimate, suggestive, seen clearly and then suddenly gone.

'So are you going to do the job or what?' Bertha asked.

6

Des had woken with the hunger back again. A sweat and some half-muffled dream where Miranda, armed with a knife, walked naked among high-rise towers. It put him off his breakfast. He stumbled out to his car and thought how awful the street looked with litter strewn everywhere. Des didn't see the sun was up until he hit the expressway heading into town. There the blue haze of pollution was already building, leaving the sun an ineffectual glow. Des worked hard to throw off the ache he felt.

'Jesus, man, I got a real job now, no need to go down the bleeding Fedora, don't have to dust off my taxi licence. Get with it, Des, and sod the woman.'

But a night spent in bed with his unconscious self proved difficult to shrug off. As he got nearer the city centre, the traffic slowed to a crawl and Des began to snarl at the congestion and confusion of passers-by. 'Sex. In-your-face sex. But where the bleeding hell is it? Bet bloody Miranda's getting it all!'

He finally got out of the jam, drove too fast down a side street and then hid himself away on the top deck of a multi-storey car park.

'Just leave me alone!'

DI Errol Wilson didn't want to see Des anywhere near work. Though an old friend from way back when Des did self-defence classes, the fact that he'd become a dick made him wary of what his colleagues might say. So they met up on the footbridge that spanned the six-lane highway, the no man's land between Alpha Tower and the city centre. When Des hauled himself up the corkscrew ramp Errol was supping a Coke and seemingly counting the cars that emerged from the Queensway tunnel.

'So how many is it since you got here?'

'Must be hundreds, man, an that's barely five minutes.'

'I can think of better places to meet, like one of those trendy new bars. You could fix me up with some trendy new food and a nice ten-year malt.'

'Shit, some of my colleagues frequent those joints, they would wanna know who you were and I'm too close to promotion to admit knowing you.'

'Ah, you're losing your touch, Errol. The ladder's going to your head.'

'I'm getting older too, Des. What the fuck, we all change.'

'Well let's go down Chinatown, eh, check out Wung Li's and have a snack. Kills you quicker than fags this place.'

'OK, man, I can live with that just the once.'

Wung Li's was much like any greasy transport caff, except of course for the Chinese script. Yellow stained walls, circus posters and plastic carnations. But the food was good and the counter always gleamed. Des slumped into a corner after ordering while DI Wilson settled down with great care. They had the place to themselves, bar two Chinese guys stuffing noodles at a table by the door.

'You really are getting fussy, aren't you, Errol?'

'Look, man, I'm earning good money. I've lived most of my life in shit and I don't need or want it any more. You wanna know how much this suit cost?' Errol ran a slim brown finger down his navy blue lapel.

'Don't give me a heart attack.'

'So what gives then, Des? What's the important business?'

'The Claudette Turton murder.'

'Shit!'

A young Chinese woman brought over the food and tea, her face courteous despite the language and Errol's insistence on serviettes.

'Jesus, Des, what are you doing this for, man? This is real gutter fuckery. I mean, I get a fat pay cheque every month, an in ten year a good pension. I can fuck off to Jamaica then, be a beach bum widout a care in the world. Shit, you don't even know if you can pay the gas bill nex month. When you retire, you'll be half starved on Social Security, queuing up wid the old dears down the market for half-price stale bread!'

'Come off it, Errol, don't give me this grief. I've got enough problems.'

'Yeh, well you certainly look a mess.'

'Just give me credit, I've landed myself with a well-paid case; a few more and I might out-snoot you.'

'All you've landed is trouble, brother.'

It took some time for Des to get Errol to talk about Claudette Turton. The deep-fried spring rolls had to be tackled with extreme caution by a cop who was concerned about getting beansprout juice on his tie. Des slurped loudly and let his fingers drip with oil.

'The usual keep-it-under-your-hat disclaimer, Des, but, well, we don't really know sweet fuck all about Claudette's murderer. Her neck was broken. She had sex at some point before she died. No signs of struggle so rape doesn't look likely, though we got a DNA fix on the guy that fucked her. Being what she was, the two events may not have been related.'

'What's with this serial killer angle?'

'Inconclusive. Whores and tarts, yeh, dumped nude in the country yeh, but then the evidence seems to vary a bit.'

50

'No leads, huh, Mr Well-Paid DI?'

'You know the score, Des. Nobody's talking, no one gives a fuck. We put the heat on her pimp, it's possible, but im don't really fit, cept the guy's a real sucker.'

'Vin St James.'

'Yeh, it'll probably be my job to make sure the git doesn't get fitted up.'

'So what you reckon then, Errol?'

'There's quite a few of these cases, Des, unsolved. Most likely some sexually screwed up nut who went too far one night, is scared shitless now and won't come out of hiding for a long time. That, or some fuckery with the vice kings and, shit, we can't get much to stick on them.'

'This is it, isn't it, Errol? Like you get your fat pay cheque every month no matter what you do, catch the crims or no. But me? Jesus, they should privatize the police and bring in payment by results. Professional cops and vice kings? Cut out the cosy status quo I say!'

'You don't believe that bollocks, do you?'

'Ner, just jealous.'

'Look, Des, we go way back and I'm happy to help, but you gotta go careful on this. You're sorta green, man, and you got no back-up, no place to hide, an if it do turn out local . . . you know what I'm saying?'

'Yeh, well I guess I have been a bit don't-give-a-shit reckless lately.'

'So I see . . . and how is Miranda?'

On his way back to Argent Street, Des felt that the bubble in the spirit level was getting centred once more. He didn't know what kind of trouble he was driving into, but the fact that he was driving made him feel he was on the mend. Besides, one problem could possibly be solved. Errol had said he would have words with Miranda. Pull the wool about Des being useful to police investigations which could be seriously harmed by a court case. And Des could even pay for the windscreen now and throw in a few extra bob for compensation. *Just get her quarantined out of my mind. Concentrate on work and I'll be a happy man. Ha, ha. If only . . .*

*   *   *

If only . . . It was the question that sometimes haunted Vin St James. That letter when he was seventeen from Eustace, his dad.

Dear Vincent

We are settle now an doin well and want for you to come to England and be wid you folk. We have nice little house to keep we warm in winter an I have jus got me firs car . . .

Vin gave off a bitter smile as he parked outside the Conference Cars showroom. Yeh, if only. He maybe wouldn't have known so much about money and all the fancy trimmings of 'civilization' but shit, a country boy without pressure might be a decent thing to be. Vin carefully concealed his knife and then gave his short hair a smooth as he looked in the rear-view mirror. The grim expression of his mouth said *I ain't neva gonna give up*. That was the way it had to be, but somewhere inside, Vin wasn't so sure. He suddenly felt weary as he got out of the car and sauntered as coolly as he could up to Ross Constanza's domain.

The road outside was its usual daytime busy. Half a mile up the long straight was the Inland Port and every few minutes a container lorry trundled up or down. Vin stood looking out of the showroom window and wondered whether Ross had a design in siting his business there. Specialist cars, high-class whores, why not import/export too? The one dat succeed, dem is always the arsehole, thought Vin as he heard the clatter of leather shoes coming towards him. Ross Constanza wasn't a big guy and he looked the car salesman in his grey suit and pink striped shirt. He even feigned the chummy banter that such gits give off which makes you feel you've just had an encounter with an ice cream. But it was all show. Vin knew the stories. The junkie who lost a finger in Kathmandu. The hard-case street-fighter who got off with manslaughter over a territorial spat. The self-made wheeler-dealer who had the edge on everyone. Vin felt his stomach churn.

'Long time no see, our Vincent.'

Ross's voice echoed in the showroom. Glass vibrated behind Vin as lorries trundled past. It was disconcerting, as was the sight of big Gus, Ross's bodyguard.

'Don't take it personal, eh Vince, but Gus is going to polish up the Bentley here while we chat. Call it standard procedure, eh.'

'Guess so . . .'

As Vin stood with his back to the glass, Ross propped himself against the Bentley and sullen Gus began to smooth away. There was five foot between them and it seemed it had to stay that way. Ross's dark eyes beckoned Vin to speak.

'Yeh, glad you could see me, man.'

'You know me, Vincent. Don't like to forget my roots.'

'Well, it a tricky subject, you know, an me ain't expressin no doubt bout you, Ross, but me worried, man, an felt me had to see you.'

'I was sorry to hear about your girl, Vince. D'you need any help, like with the funeral or something?'

'No, man, it like . . . me can't figure it out, you know, how she got kill. Sometin ain't right bout it . . .'

'That's bound to be, mate, otherwise it wouldn't have happened.'

'Yeh, but, me need to know sometin, right, to put me mind at res, like me owe it to me an she.'

'What're you trying to say, Vince?'

'Shit, me jus wanna know whether she was two-timin me, out graftin on the side, mebbe wuckin feh you.'

'Vincent, come on, I'm not into that and you should know it. Jesus, man, you think I might use street girls, tenquid blowjobs and all that crap? Come on, what is this I'm standing next to, eh? A bleeding Bentley, Vince!'

'Me a tell you, Ross, don't tek offence. Dere was rumour, dat is all, some a dese rich shits dey like a common tart an, well man, me jus wanna know whether Claudette she was fuckin me aroun.'

'She probably was, Vincent, but not with me. I get to hear the rumours too, pal, and the way I heard it, your loving woman had another fella, like she must have had one hell of an appetite that bird.'

Two lorries thundered past. The road, the glass, his whole back seemed to shudder as Ross's words echoed away across the flash, second-hand cars.

'You kiddin me, man.'

'That's what I heard, mate.'

'Shit, me can't . . . it ain't. Shit . . .'

Vin went away stunned. He barely knew he was walking to his car. All he could feel was a strange void, a straining emptiness that he knew was about to collapse. He had been conned! As he got into his car, he didn't see Ross and Gus looking at him through sky-reflecting glass. Even without lorries thundering past, he had no way of knowing what Ross said.

'You better get Scobie onto this, Gus. Give it a few days, yeh, and don't make it obvious. Scobie can pick a fight or something, but our Vincent, well, he could do with some disability benefit.'

*　　*　　*

So Des was back in the doorway of the Lime Tree, just like that night when the rain made puddles in Claudette's eyes. But Des wasn't feeling quite so panicky. He was on the job now. He had some kind of protection. The last time he'd spent any time there was at one of Stevie Kitson's dos and he'd been with Miranda. Bad scene. He'd kind of conned her down with overtures of 'let's be friends' but really he was trying to persuade her back to him. It had ended in shouts and tears. So Des kept away. The Lime Tree was the 'Slime' from then on.

But now he was going through the well-worn doors again, scanning the nicotine walls and coming face to face with brassy Eileen, the landlady queen.

'Well, Jesus Mary, look what the cat dragged in.'

'You're looking as gorgeous as ever, Eileen, like you've just come in from milking the cows.'

'I don't know if I should take that as a compliment, Des, though I think it's better than being a bedraggled mouse.'

'Certainly is. So how's it going? Still the cops' favourite mother figure?'

'Come to my bosom still.'

'And what a bosom.'

'And out of bounds to you. Still whisky, is it, Des?'

'Yeh. Is Bertha Turton around, d'you know?'

'Surely, just around the corner.'

Des was rather surprised. Bertha looked different. She wore a long floral dress and make-up that had somehow dissolved the pale weariness of her face. Bertha was dolled up and Des was quite impressed.

'Bit early in the day, isn't it, to be thinking of going out on the town?'

'I was pissed off. A bit of war paint can make you feel better.'

'Yeh, little tricks for depressed hearts, eh.'

'God, don't go on like that, Des.'

'Sorry.'

'You're definitely in then?'

'Yep.'

'OK, but I want to be kept up-to-date, right? And I want to know everything you find out.'

'Sure.'

Des eased himself round to the seat next to Bertha. He took a whiff of perfume and started to feel strange. Being so close to such a display of femininity was a distraction. Des strained to remain focused.

'So, how about we start with Vin?'

'Small-time trash, Des. He's a likeable guy and I mean he really cared for our Claudette but, you know, he's a bit slow on the uptake, got no drive. Vin just wants to drift and Claudette hated that.'

Des was vaguely aware of a similar experience but he brushed it aside. 'No big arguments or bones of contention?'

'Not that I know of, but I wouldn't know for sure. I have to say, Claudette was no angel. She was headstrong and not a little sly.'

'I wonder where she got that from?'

'Des, come on, we were going along fine.'

'Forgive me. Cynicism, it comes out every so often like an unwanted fart. So Vin isn't out of the frame. What about other pals?'

Bertha urged Des to check on a couple of girlfriends, but there was little else he noted. And by then Des's mind was beginning to wander. It was over there, by the horse brasses on the wall, where they had sat. A stab of pain hit him and he shuddered. He knew he should never have seen her that last time. Places, they get covered in all sorts of things, like the hidden smells that dogs sniff. Des tried to pull himself around; he had an inkling Bertha was saying something interesting.

'. . . On the game myself, God, must be twenty years ago

now. So I knew the score, could tell her what a bloody fool she was but couldn't really argue against it.'

Des struggled for words. Bertha put a hand on his thigh and smiled.

'You don't have to say anything, luv. I'm a survivor and don't ask for any sympathy.'

Des noticed she had a gold ring on each finger and that her skin was beginning to close around them. He too tried to smile and began to wonder what was going on.

'You still with that Miranda, then?'

'Nah.'

'Ceceline said she was a stuck-up bitch.'

'Ceceline would.'

'Fancy something a bit more posh, did you? Satin sheets and silk pyjamas?'

'It was hardly that, but why not anyway?'

'Come on, Des, you're supposed to be savvy, I bet you just got bleeding used.'

'Huh, you tell me a deal where people aren't used?'

Bertha looked Des in the eyes, those brown bullet eyes that made him shrink. She patted his thigh before taking her hand away, and then she gave a wry smile.

'You're not so likely to be used, Des, when you're the one who walks.'

7

Why Chinatown? Des found himself thinking as he drove around Small Heath looking for Vin St James. How many Chinese are there that every big city should have one? Why not Pakistanitown or Punjabville or the Azaad Kashmir quarter? What is it with these Chinese folks that the top bods in the Town Hall and the tourists just love em so much? Des was going up the Stratford Road at the time, checking out the balti houses and Islamic bookshops that lined the street. He was on the job and feeling good. It was a bit like he was seeing the city for the first time. He stopped at a set of traffic lights and got come-on eyes from an Asian girl in tight pants. 'Yeh,' he said with near enthusiasm as he then turned left into Golden Hillock Road and thought of minarets in fields of ripened corn. Vin hadn't been seen at the Lime Tree for over a week. Nor had he been at the house he shared with Claudette. But Des had got a sort of lead at the Earl. A group of dope-smoking brethren suggested he try the Vine. It was Vin's regular circuit and now Des was doing it, making straightforward progress as a prospective customer looking for a high.

The Vine was a little bit of Kingston amid the nation states of Small Heath (one of the smallest, along with the principality of South Yemen). It was there that he struck lucky. He met Tone, one of the Iwah crew, who Des had once taught self-defence. Tone had gone down the tubes quite a lot since he'd last seen him. His face was pinched thin and there was a chemical look to his complexion. But he remembered Des and was happy to help. Out came the mobile phone. Des played it straighter this time, told Tone to mention a business deal and the name Bertha. With Tone overdoing the recommendations, Vin had to accept and he named a time and place.

'Many thanks, Tone, I ought to get a mobile.'

'E-ssential, man, gotta keep ahead of the game.'

'Don't it piss you off, beeping and stuff?'

'Look, if me a block up me don't hear it anyway; an if me, you know, doin it, me ansa it feh a laugh. All the res a the time it business, man.'

'I guess, just like the boss of ICI.'

'Yeh man, you can bet the guy im get stone an fuck im women an run im business the res a the time, jus like me.'

'You could be up there, Tone.'

'Me a knockin on the door, man.'

Heaven's door, thought Des as he got into his car and drove off to see Vin.

It had to be sign of a paranoid man. A cul-de-sac, lost and forgotten in the arse end of town. There were a couple of derelict workshops on one side of him and the unbroken back end of a factory on the other. Des got out of the car, but could see no one else. The factory brick wall was lavishly daubed with unintelligible graffiti. Looking back at the street he'd come down, all Des could see were galvanized railings and some sort of dumping ground for dead engines behind. He kicked brick detritus aimlessly and began to wonder whether he was in a trap or just ditched once again. Then he heard the voice from behind the fence.

'You ain't carryin, are you?'

Des turned. He couldn't see anyone. 'Er, no. Hey, where the hell are you?'

A trilby then rose above the fence, followed by Vin's worn and suspicious face.

'Jesus, is this a joke?' Des said, shuffling his feet.

'Me know you, ain't it? We done business some time in a past.'

'Sure, man, you know me.'

'So who you a wuckin feh?'

'No one. Look, we can't talk like this. You want to come out? I've got no axe to grind with you.'

Vin continued to give Des some heavy scrutiny and then nodded his head. 'You come to me, man. The plank wid the mark on it dere, it push through.'

Heaving a big sigh, Des moved over, pushed and made an opening. He got a glimpse of a canal behind. It was a bit of a squeeze and when he'd finally got most of himself through, he suddenly found himself intimate with a knife.

'So who you wuckin feh?'

Finally clear of the gap in the fence, Des was now backed up against the boards. The knife was five inches from his throat. Vin looked coldly determined to keep the situation that way.

'Come on, Vin, what is this?'

'Who you wuckin feh?'

It became too much. Des felt violated. He darted his head suddenly to look down the towpath. Vin's eyes did the same and so missed the left uppercut that thundered to his jaw. Des had the knife in no time and a foot on Vin's chest too.

'You stupid bugger. I came here to talk, maybe even help you. Sod it, man, no one pulls a knife on me!'

Vin groaned. Des stooped down, pulled Vin up and propped him against the fence. He looked around. Deserted. On one side, ancient factories. Des could see plants growing out of the crumbling walls. The towpath side was bordered by fencing and, further down, coils of razor wire. Des looked at the gloomy water and shivered with the sudden feeling of fear that he might fall in.

'Shit, you pack a bleedin punch.'

'So you ain't dead, are you, Vin? I mean, do I look like I'm about to cause you grievous harm?'

'Me don't trust nuttin an no one at the moment, man.'

'Just check this, right. I'm a private investigator. I've been hired to find out about Claudette's death. All I want to do is ask you some questions, off the record, confidential, no comebacks – however you want it.'

'Huh, waste you time, me don't know nuttin bout it. Wish me did.'

'Come on, why're you acting so scared?'

'Heat, man. Me was close to the fire, an some fucker out dere's gonna tink me was the one wid the matches.'

'Were you?'

'Course not! She jus went out to she fren. Dat's all me know bout it till she turn up dead.'

'And who was the friend?'

'A tart call Pauline, but she neva went dere.'

'Never went or never got there?'

'Me dunno, man. Shit, me don't even fucking care now. Me reckon the bitch she was jus shaftin me.'

Des got a little niggle of emotion at the word shaftin. He gripped hard onto Vin's knife and thought about giving the fence a stab.

'No ideas who with?'

'Me ain't neva really hurt anyone, man, but if me knew dat . . .'

'So why're you so scared?'

'Me tell you, man! The pigs, whoever did feh Claudette, shit, whoever Claudette was mixed up wid.'

'You got anyone in mind?'

'It ain't the sorta ting me'd like to know.'

Vin's shifty eyes seemed to imply that it was the sort of thing he might know, but he didn't want to admit it, and for sure he wasn't going to tell Des. He stared down at the parched grass he was sitting on and left the next move up to Des. Des didn't have one. He tried to think what to do – get heavy, get physical – but his heart wasn't in it. Vin's hat had come off when he'd socked him and now Des looked down at a shaven head. It looked vulnerable and tired. He sensed that maybe Vin was only out to survive and just wanted to be left alone. Des sympathized.

'Shit. This place gives me the creeps,' he said and moved towards the hole in the fence. 'If you come up with anything you think I should know, get in touch, eh, there might be dosh in it.'

'What bout me blade, man?'

'I'll throw it back over the fence.'

And so Des squeezed out from one dump of a place and into another. He unlocked his car and then remembered the knife. He got it over the fence OK, but too well. He heard the splash but didn't wait for the curses that were sure to follow.

*   *   *

Jerry had the sickness. He sat on the sofa, arms folded, and stared at the bare walls opposite. He saw nothing and rarely did a thought cross his mind. Inertia. Pure, don't-give-a-toss inertia. He could do it for hours on end. It was the usual story. Cut adrift and feeling too tired to fight it. Few people knew how much hard work there is in being workless, how much energy is needed to stay afloat when there's no support and the only outlook is down. Jerry had spent days toiling with nothing. He'd had many fitful nights too, slipping in and out of revenge dreams, eyes behind the sights of a sniper gun, killing off all the shits in the world. Jerry was wrecked and hadn't even managed to call on Mary. But that was about to change. There were noises on the fire escape and he heard the outside door creak open.

Mary stepped brightly into the living room. She was wearing a thin cotton blouse and a long skirt, and the way the light hit her, Jerry thought she wore nothing else. He squirmed a little with hunger. She slumped down beside him on the sofa and waved a brown envelope, wafting cool air around them.

'Jerry, the day is glorious and you're looking like a dead rat in a hole.'

'Yeh. F-Feel like one.'

'So what's the matter, huh?'

'You know . . . nothing, the b-big fucking nothing out there, and the m-malice it holds.' Jerry tried to smile.

'Boring self-pity. You should've come down to see me instead of moping.'

Jerry felt a little confused by Mary's sudden breezy appearance, and ashamed too for being so morbid. He tried to rise to the occasion.

'Are you t-trying to cool me d-down, or are you going to show m-me what's in that envelope?' he said with his head somewhat averted – he could see Mary's breasts beneath the purple flowers of her blouse and he wasn't sure how to react. That was the thing about Mary, she kept coming out with things and you were never sure where she was at.

'I wasn't going to tell anyone, but, well it's hard to resist and I reckon it's safe to tell you.'

'S-So what is this?'

A slyly smiling Mary gave the envelope to Jerry and suggested he look inside. He pulled out a couple of large black and white photographs. Two people having sex, doggy style, with the man at the back straining his head up in contorted ecstasy. Somewhat amazed, Jerry couldn't work it out but then noticed the blurred edge of a curtain at the side of the pictures.

'H-Have I got this right? Y-You took these? I mean, you took these through a w-window like a p-peeping tom?'

'Awful, isn't it?'

'B-But, this isn't portfolio stuff . . .'

'Sort of. Well, I'm getting paid for them which is more than I can say about most of the other work I've done.'

'W-What's it for, is the b-bloke two-timing or something?'

'I'm not sure about that. This woman I met down the Lime Tree, Claudette, you may have seen her around. We were chatting, I said I was trying to set up as a photographer and she said she'd like to teach this bloke a lesson.'

'Yeh, I think I've seen her around.'

'God, it was scary doing it, Jerry, but exciting, you know. I got quite turned on. I was printing a few up the other day and it brought it all back.'

'So, d-did you get paid?'

'Half. I'm expecting the rest but she hasn't been around the past while.'

'Jesus, M-Mary, you're certainly full of surprises.'

She looked at Jerry then, straight in the eyes. There was a glint within them, a glint Jerry hadn't seen much of recently.

'Hey,' she said, 'let's go out for a walk.'

'Shit, I d-don't know . . .'

'So how is it with you and that Wanda then?'

'W-Why do you ask?'

'Well, I haven't seen her around, that's all.'

Jerry and Mary were sitting on the grass down at Sparkhill Park. The sun was out and so were the people, dotted around the acres of green away from the relentless traffic. The benches by the driveway were full of OAPs. A few young men kicked a ball about while a circle of Sikhs played cards by the rose bushes.

64

'I g-guess it's m-more or less folded. I haven't w-wanted to go round and see her. No spark left, I guess, just habit.'

'Yeh, the way they go, relationships.'

'Y-You know I want y-you.'

Jerry thought he could say that then, in the park, in a public place, as though the context took away the import of his words. But Mary was grinning; she leaned over close and looked into Jerry's eyes.

'Say it again.'

'W-What? I w-want you?'

'God, your stutter drives me wild.'

And then Mary kissed him, a kiss that was long and searching, almost a tongue fuck as she sat astride him and spread her skirt over him.

'Come on, Jerry, let's!'

'D-Do y-y-you th-think –'

'Shush! Put your hands under my skirt.'

All the seediness that had brooded within him for days suddenly went. Jerry began to feel that he was in the sea and about to drown. He looked around and saw the complacent faces of the old folks on the benches and the surly youths thumping leather. A toddler waddling along the drive with her mum was looking straight at Jerry. He wanted to shout, to wave his arms and scream out that he was in trouble, but the waters proved more alluring than fear. He slid his hands down into silky softness and found the wet place of his dreams.

'Oh, Jerry, that is good . . . Now, try to get your jeans down.'

'B-But –'

'No one can see anything, we just look like we're being playful.'

But the toddler was staring now and seemed to sense something was going on. And a poker-faced old lady was certainly looking hard at them. But Jerry couldn't stop the pull of the waves. He carefully eased down his jeans and Mary sank herself down. He closed his eyes and let himself be absorbed by the lapping sea. He was vaguely aware of Mary's face above the water and, beyond that, a distorted, malignant tree but then the climax came. Jerry writhed and choked and finally opened his eyes to a disconcerting sky.

*   *   *

Several hours later, Des drove Bertha in the direction of Burma Road. His mind was beginning to buzz, and it wasn't about a certain someone. He'd picked Bertha up at the Fedora and had encountered an almost animated Wayne.

'Bleedin hell, Des, you ought to pack up the job more often. This place nearly came alive.'

'What's happening?'

'Another customer besides Dick, Bertha over there, and two phone calls for you. The dreaded M rang, said she was dropping the charges but to expect a bill through the post. Then that posh woman rang. She said she was "going ahead", whatever that means, and the cheque's on the way. I mean, Des, we haven't had such action in months!'

Des smiled to himself and then caught sight of the milk crates on the corner of Burma Road. No old men sat on them, but placards were hanging on the railings. Des looked over at Bertha.

'Could be another suspect there,' he said.

'What? The holier-than-thous?'

'One way to get the girls off the street. You know, these religious nutter types, they can be extreme.'

'Don't forget, Des, I'm reformed. I might even agree with them.'

'Yeh, well it's like dope, they're shit scared to legalize it.'

Des went down Burma Road, took a few more turns in

the backstreets and finally pulled up outside an Edwardian terraced house, last known home of Claudette Turton.

'You're sure Vin won't be around?'

'He's frightened, Bertha, gone to ground.'

'I guess he wouldn't want to see me anyway.'

Bertha took out her key to the house and they went inside. Darkness was beginning to fall and so they switched on the lights as they went in each room. It all seemed very neat and tidy.

'S'pose the police have had a good poke round.'

'And you can bet that as soon as he heard, Vin flushed the place over.'

Downstairs consisted of a front room, living room and kitchen. Des and Bertha went snooping round all the furniture, cushions and kitchenware but found nothing of interest.

'Strange,' Des muttered, 'going through someone else's house.'

'Bit of a waste of time.'

'You don't get much sense of what the two of them were like.'

'Mmmm, guess some of this stuff should come to me.'

'Would you want it?'

'Nah, I got the things I . . .'

Bertha briefly took hold of Des's hand and squeezed, but Des found that her face gave little away.

'You OK?'

'God, let's get it over with.'

Upstairs, too, seemed totally unpromising. A front bed-room where the couple had slept and another where Claudette plied her trade. Both tidied up and clean along with the bathroom. *Not any kind of personal scent. Not a sniff of dramas that once went on. Too unreal. Claudette already seems a memory kept alive in her mother's mind.*

Des watched Bertha looking through her daughter's clothes. Her looks may have waned with time, her body lost its symmetry, but he could see attractiveness there. He liked it. Beauty with character, not glamour; subtle pleasures maybe, post-menopause. Des pulled himself up abruptly. Business, his mind asserted, strictly business!

'I'll just do another check around.'

Des again went round the too-tidy house. Two things came to his attention. In the front room, behind the door, Des noticed a clown print. Not exactly the same as the other one that had witnessed a small humiliation of his own. It was similar enough, though, to send a ripple of unease through him and a desire to thump its inane face. Des moved quickly away. He'd failed to check the back yard. On opening the rear door, there seemed little to be bothered about. In the fading light he could see paving stones swamped by weeds. A rotary drier collapsed and rusting by the back fence. There were, however, two bulging black plastic bags by the gate. Rats had gnawed their way into both. Refraining from breathing in, Des got down on his haunches and prodded around at the spewing mess with a pen. Potato peels and eggshells, unidentifiable slime and fag ash, but also scraps of paper. Gingerly, he tried to ease a few out of the filth. A shopping list, a few columns of figures, till receipts . . . Bertha appeared at the back door.

'I reckon I might have found something, Des.'

He looked up.

'In one of Claudette's jackets, stuffed right down in the pocket.'

*   *   *

It was completely dark when Des began to drive Bertha back to her home. He was feeling pleased with himself and certain things in his life were beginning to seem long gone. He put on an Abdullah Ibrahim tape and allowed his fingers to play a tune on the steering wheel.

'So read the note again, Bertha.'

'My special friends call me Bee.'

'B is for boss don't forget.'

'Huh. OK – "Sorry about this. I tried to ring but couldn't get you. I'm out of town for a few days so you won't be able to reach me. Let me know as soon as you can about the VIP . . ." and it's signed "G".'

'What you reckon then?'

'Well, she was playing around, the naughty girl, as Vin suspected, whoever G is.'

'Sounds possible. Then again, it could be just an innocuous arrangement. What about VIP?'

'No idea.'

'I suppose that could be just a personal joke, you know, like people have names for their genitalia. Or it could be pointing to a scam.'

'Find out, Des. What am I paying you for?'

Bertha lived on the third floor of a ten-storey block of flats some half a mile to the east of Argent Street. Des pulled into the car park and waited for Bertha to get out.

'You coming up for a coffee, Des?'

'Nah, I think I'll give it a miss if you don't mind.'

'I won't bite, you know.'

'I dunno about that, and that worries me, you being my client and all.'

'So what if I did bite, Des? I'm pretty good at knowing where and how to do it. I mean, we're both well grown-up now and, if I'm not mistaken, you, like me, are pretty hungry.'

'Don't say that.'

'I know what it's like. I've been caught out too, hooked on a drug and suffered withdrawal.'

'Bertha, this doesn't feel right.'

'Don't worry, it'll be fine.'

'Oh, I dunno . . .'

Bertha smiled. It was a warm smile and appealingly accentuated by many lines.

'By the way, Des, do you have a name for yours?'

8

Flat 34 was a celebration of the pink frill. Everywhere you looked in the various pink-painted rooms, the scalloped adornments were there. On valanced curtains, cushions, drapes and mirror frames. As mock flowers standing tall on green canes. But for a full realization of Bertha's taste, the bedroom was the place to see. Pillowcase and counterpane, pink frilly canopy above the bed and a huge foaming lampshade. All this amid deep magenta walls, pink carpet and bed. Des McGinlay lay on this bed, lit up a fag and tried to think about the mess he was getting in to. He'd let himself be seduced. The implications were scary, the complications too awful to consider. So Des gave up thinking and sank back down to his feelings. To his surprise, they were good. The first time he'd writhed with uncertainty in Bertha's arms and felt guilty over Miranda, but the second time that night, that time he'd really made love, and he'd felt great because of it. Bertha was true to her word. She knew where and how to do the things that made Des feel almost himself again. She entered the bedroom with a tray of coffee and scrambled eggs on toast.

'You shouldn't still be in bed, Des, there's work to be done.'

'I hate eggs for breakfast.'

'Don't expect me to know everything about you yet.'

Bertha set the tray down on the bedside table. She wore a

see-through shift, pink of course, and she let it slip off her shoulders as she lay next to Des. But Des, though appreciative of her body, didn't really notice. He was still wincing over the word 'yet'. It sounded so menacing, a threat that he might be swallowed up. But it was a titillating threat. Despite the flouncy cheapness of all the trimmings, there was an allure to Bertha's view of home, a sense of snuggling, an oblivious passion that Des could submit to as an escape from the hard-edged world. Des saw then that the frilliness was indicative of a womb, Bertha's womb, beginning to open as she rubbed herself against his thigh.

'Bleeding hell, Bertha, I have got to work, you know.'

'What difference will half an hour make now?'

'You never know.'

'And so won't miss . . .'

Bertha's tongue went down to his ribs and onwards like a trickle of warm honey. Des became lost once more in pinkness, moist and alive . . .

It was midday before he was out on the road, though he wasn't too sure what he was doing there. He had the names and addresses of two prostitutes who were friendly with Claudette, but he was still woozy with Bertha and couldn't think straight. First it was, *Well that's got one back on Miranda*, and then, *But Bertha, she's like a bad drug. Too good to refuse; too dangerous to know*. He was elated and pissed off at the same time. Des decided a snifter was needed before he followed any leads. So, it was down to the real world where the ghosts of murder victims and ex-lovers mingled with the everyday punters. Des propped up the bar and smiled at Eileen.

'Here's to foot and mouth and mad, mad cows!'

'Scrapie with pork scratchings!'

'Love it – here's a battery chicken in your eye!'

'And a crate of veal to go with it!'

'The way it goes, eh Eileen, down the tubes.'

'Yep, and all you can try to do is go happy. Speaking of which, you almost seem happy yourself.'

'Don't be conned; a temporary aberration I'm sure.'

'But that Miranda's finally gone where all the mad cows go?'

'Well, I dunno. Can you believe what the authorities say?'

'That sandwich you're eating is not mad, Des!'

He grinned at Eileen. He'd forgotten how well they got on. But then that was the nature of her job and nothing special.

'So tell me, what's your view on Claudette's death?'

'Jesus, Des, I don't know.'

'What did you make of her, though? She was in here quite a bit.'

'Well, she spread herself around, you know, liked chatting. She'd rub shoulders with anyone at the bar.'

'What, for any purposes?'

'Oh yes, she was always on the lookout, you could tell. Who's who and what they've got to offer.'

'Anyone in particular?'

'I wouldn't have noticed. It gets too busy in here, but it makes you think.'

'What?'

'You know, the creep who killed her. He could be a customer. I could be serving the bastard beer!'

The first name on Des's list was Sharon Mason. He found her at her home in the red-light district and she was happy to talk. With Bertha's recommendation behind him, Des walked into a kitchen with shopping on the table and toys on the floor. Sharon was a slim young woman with mousy hair. She had cute, youthful looks that Des guessed might help with her work. But Sharon was clocked off and determined to be her normal self.

'Yeh, I was pretty friendly with her. You know, we hung around the same pitch at night, had a laugh, looked out for each other.'

'You got any idea about her death? See anything funny?'

'Nothing really. We'd come across some weird johns and piss-taking kids and stuff, but that's kind of normal. There was nothing scary that I remember, nothing we had really bad feelings about.'

'You don't think it was a lone nutcase?'

'I doubt it, she wasn't even on the game that night.'

'So what do you think?

'I dunno. You know, you think about it because it could've been me, but . . .'

Sharon began to sort out the shopping. She did it in a very ordered and meticulous way and Des wondered if she was like that with her punters. The thought made him shudder.

'What's the talk among the girls?'

'Well, there's a feeling she was up to something, like she was doing something on the side and it blew up in her face.'

'No ideas?'

'Money, it had to do with making money. That's all she ever talked about, making money and getting away.'

'With Vin?'

Sharon made a face. 'Vin was in the doghouse,' she said.

'So who?'

'Sod knows. You're gonna have to talk to Pauline about that.'

Nothing much there. Des left Sharon to her domesticity. House to clean, meals to prepare and kids to organize.

Pauline lived two streets down. Des took the opportunity for a short stroll in the sunshine and the rare chance to indulge in feeling good. *A lover and a job all in one day.*

Can't be bad. The feeling didn't last. Pauline wasn't at home. A chunky guy with a huge black moustache was. Des should've seen the potential for trouble, the way the guy squared up to him and glared, but Des was in the pink and slack because of it.

'Hi there,' Des said with a smirk. 'I'm McGinlay, a private investigator, and I want to speak to Pauline.'

The man in the door didn't reply, merely intensified his glare and somehow filled out the doorway more.

'You get me, yeh? Pauline? I mean, that moustache, there is a mouth under it, isn't there?'

'Huh, snoopin after our Pauline, are yer? Fuckin private dick! We've had the soddin pigs round half a dozen times and I'll be fucked if we want you!'

'There is a mouth.'

'Eh?'

'Forget it. Look, I don't want to speak to you –'

'No one speaks to our Pauline without my say-so.'

'Come on, chill out. This heavy macho thing, it's movie stuff,' Des quipped. It was one quip too many.

'Fuckin smartarse!' The man lifted up a slab hand and propped it on Des's chest. 'Well you just check this, dick-face. No –' and the guy began to push '– scumbag – little – snooper – comes knocking – on my – fuckin door – without good reason – or a fuckin invitation!'

Des suddenly found himself on the pavement, pressed up against a car. Only then did he begin to get seriously concerned and to think of protecting himself. Too late.

'An just in case the message hasn't got home' – the guy pulled back his arm – 'fuckin this might make it so!'

Des saw the fist coming but blocked to no avail. A solid thump hit him in the solar plexus. Des bent double, gasping for air. The steak sandwich in his stomach began to get ideas about reincarnation. Des teetered away on wobbly legs, and found a tree to hold on to.

'An don't fuckin well come back!' he heard as he sought to breathe without retching at the same time. After a while, when most of the nausea had gone, Des began to feel angry. Not so much with the thug as with himself. 'Slack,' he muttered to himself. 'Unprofessional. Five minutes on the job and I'm almost fucked!' He picked himself up and gingerly went on his way.

*   *   *

Even on the third floor there was no horizon to see. Houses, factories and blocks of flats. For many years, Bertha had barely given the view a second thought. It was just there, ugly and to be ignored. But now she was looking, not seeing, and thinking that maybe one day she could be an observer of the sea instead. One day, the hidden horizon and those she knew with no horizons could be left behind. There was hope. It sat in a pile on the sofa like an unexpected guest. Five thousand pounds. It wasn't enough to get you to the sea, to allow you to stay, but such a sum could well create more, and so hope was justified. Bertha left the window and sat down by the money. But how to make it grow? She had few financial skills; she didn't know about much other than typing and that job she'd done so long ago. But maybe there was opportunity. What she once did, so did her daughter, and whatever Claudette was involved with, so Bertha could seek to exploit. But how? The phone quietly beeped its way into her thoughts.

'Yes.'

'Bertha, you didn't give me any warning, did you?'

'That you, Des?'

'Yeh, a rather pissed off Des.'

'What's happened, sweetheart?'

'You didn't tell me about the walrus that minds Pauline.'

'Have you got hurt or something?'

'Nah, wounded pride mostly. But this git, he's built like a tank and fires howitzers if you try to get past him.'

'I thought you could handle yourself, Des.'

'Yeh well . . . a bit out of practice, and softened up by you.'

'We had a nice time, though.'

'Something I'll have to sort out, the pain and the pleasure of the job.'

'Ha, don't know if I like the sound of that.'

'Don't worry, but it would help if you could set up a meet with Pauline minus the bodyguard.'

'I'll fix that, but are you sure you're OK? I wouldn't like you to get hurt.'

'Isn't that what you're paying me for?'

As she put the phone down, Bertha smiled. *That makes a change, paying the man.* She picked up the money and wrapped it ready for hiding. The plan was on its way. Bertha smiled again. Quite a coup for a secretary. A secret second life with a man to meet her every need. And, if the plan goes well, a way out to greater riches, an escape from the concrete sprawl to sensuous pleasures by the sea. Bertha pulled herself up sharp. She was fantasizing too far ahead. Yet she knew her daughter, had her suspicions and if proved right, there could well be more money to come. Bertha took the pile of notes into the bedroom, removed a few and then stashed them away. *Tomorrow, new clothes and moving forward to past glories and maybe even sweet revenge . . .*

*   *   *

'I'm sorry about Barry, really. It's just, well we've had a lot of hassle since Claudette was killed. What with the cops and all the talk, it's buggered up my work and Barry's dead pissed off about it. You must've been the last straw.'

'Huh, cept he seemed to want to break my back.'

'He can be a vicious bastard, I know. I really am sorry.'

Pauline was a small shapely woman with short black hair and an angular face where chin and cheekbones stood out strong. A mask-like face, never changing and never giving anything away. Des didn't like Pauline but then Barry might've had something to do with that.

'I could do without the crocodile tears.'

'Your snout's in dirty waters, Des, what d'you expect?'

'Some bleeding sympathy for Claudette. Some desire to help catch her killer.'

'We'll do what we think it's safe to do. You just rubbed Barry up the wrong way.'

'Yeh, well remind me to get even.'

Des was back at the Earl with Pauline. A slack afternoon where the soundless TV flickered and two kids clattered pool at the end of the bar. Pauline lit up a cigarette, her waxy face immobile while her eyes were on full alert. A sharp tart, Des thought, a survivor and unlikely to end up with a snapped neck.

'So what's the view on Claudette's death?'

'Come on, I don't know anything more than anyone else. They say she was on her way to come and see me but I never knew bout it.'

'She didn't arrange it?'

'Course not. It was just some fuckin excuse she gave to Vin.'

'The sort of excuse she'd use to go and see her fancy bloke?'

'Maybe.'

'Some bloke whose name begins with G?'

'My, you are the detective.'

'And G is for –?'

'The going rate is fifty quid.'

'Jesus . . .'

'You're using up my valuable work time.'

'After what Barry did, you owe me!'

'I reckon I should make something out of this mess. I've lost enough days' work.'

Des sighed. There's no way you argue with a woman like Pauline. He wearily reached into his back pocket. A sudden stab of pain hit him, but it wasn't physical and it wasn't Bertha. A holiday, a year or more back. Des could see it. Him and Miranda on a beach beneath tamarisk trees. A bottle of wine and knowing smiles. A bloody lifetime away.

'OK, here's the fifty. Spit out the poison, eh.'

'His name's Gary Marlow. I don't know much about him, cept he was young, flash and sold coke to rich pricks round the hotels and stuff.'

'Great. And was Claudette hot on him?'

'Don't know bout that but they'd got something together.'

'How'd they meet?'

'I never did work that out.'

'And where is Gary now?'

'South America, I wouldn't be surprised.'

'You reckon he did it?'

'Bloody hell, what do you want for your fifty quid?'

Des sighed again. What did he want? He wanted a tamarisk tree, a bottle of wine and one of those knowing smiles.

9

It was his only way into the hotel scene. A friend of Miranda's who he didn't want to see. Des could only say What the hell? and insist to himself the worst was over. The High Park was four star. A modern cube faced with pink concrete and thin windows. A real bollock of an eyesore. Des eased into the cream and brown foyer and confronted the obligatory plastic smile.

'I'm looking for Vera May Partington.'

'Yes? One of the chambermaids. I believe she's working at the moment.'

'This is urgent, a family matter that can't wait.'

'Well, I suppose I could put a call out for her.'

Des put on his own big grin. The receptionist looked about eighteen and had susceptible eyes.

'Do it,' he soothed. 'It's your job, eh, make connections, help the world move on its way. I'll be in the lounge.'

He settled into an armchair a whole room away from a group of blue suits taking coffee and spreadsheets. Des breathed deeply. This was the first friend of Miranda he'd met since the bust-up. He hadn't wanted to see any of them ever again. But Vera May, maybe she wouldn't be too bad. She never did have her finger on the button. Was writing some sort of novel apparently and working part time to make ends meet. When did they ever?

*

'My God, it's you!' gasped Vera May.

'Couldn't be anyone else.'

'I thought it was going to be my dad or something.'

'A more interesting alternative, I hope.'

'Des, it's been some time.'

Vera May actually wore a black dress and a white apron. Des was quite taken with it; in fact, he was quite taken with her. She sat down next to him and Des suddenly became aware of a difference. No Miranda now, so he could fancy Vera May as much as he liked. There were compensations. And she was attractive. A smooth, flat face and a curled smile. A slim body with large breasts which seemed to tilt her forward. Des felt quite relaxed.

'It's nice to see you, Vera May.'

'Yes, I suppose so, but awfully unexpected. You're the last person I'd've thought to see.'

'Funny how that gets said. We see all kinds of strangers every day, but the people we know we don't expect.'

'You're . . . you're not here about –?'

'She's dead and buried as far as I'm concerned.' Des wondered whether he'd said it too affirmatively.

'Oh, so . . .' Vera May began to shift uncomfortably in her seat.

'Don't worry, it's my job. I'm here to snoop about the seedy side of hotel life.'

'You mean you're still doing investigating?'

'Yeh, and I'm looking for a line on getting a snort of cocaine.'

'I don't know what's going on, Des.'

'You always were the last to know.'

Des filled in the bewildered Vera May with the broad details of the case. It still didn't seem to click with her, like this was some elaborate, dubious tale Des was spinning. But finally, perhaps just deciding to go along with it, she suggested Des talk to the security manager. Vera May made a phone call at reception to arrange for him to come down, then returned and sat back down with disbelieving eyes.

'You've never been propositioned for dope or whatever?'

'No. In the daytime you hardly see the guests. It's the male staff who always proposition me. With bedrooms everywhere, their heads are full of sex.'

'You still going out with that geezer John?'

'No, we bust up a while ago.'

'Sign of the times.'

'We're still good friends, in fact he's still living in the house. I think he wants me back.'

'Sounds a bit tricky.'

'It is, because I'm in love with someone else.'

'Sounds quick.'

'Yes, and stupid. I think this guy is raving mad.'

'Different.'

'Oh, I don't know, I couldn't help myself. He's charismatic and I was on the rebound. I definitely reckon he's a full-blown schizophrenic.'

'You don't seem too worried.'

'Whatever. Fate's as good as anything these days for guiding your life.'

'Well, Vera May, you look good on it.' And Des gave a beaming smile.

They promised to meet up for a drink. Des was tempted but thought they never would. She drifted off when the security guy turned up. Des turned his attention to Mr Parkes, another blue suit, and this one, he could tell, was an ex-cop.

'I'm not a great believer in private investigators, Mr McGinlay, but since I'm private now, I guess there are grounds for co-operation.'

'Discretion assured,' Des said, 'if you've any worries.'

'So what's the problem?'

Des gave an outline of his investigations and this seemed

to impress the thin-faced Parkes. He twirled a gold pen in his fingers, his brown eyes staring unblinking at Des.

'Now. We have this Gary Marlow toting gear to hotel clientele and a pro who was desperate for big money. Next step, what are the hotel angles?'

'What are the police doing?'

'Checking out lone perverts, I believe.'

'Mmm, well, you'll see no illicit dealings here, not that I've discovered anyway.'

'Gary Marlow hasn't a reputation?'

'I haven't heard, but I know these things go on.'

'Yeh?'

'Someone on the inside of the hotel, a porter or other member of staff acts as a go-between. So if a guest wants something special, the member of staff makes his connection outside and sets up a deal. It's more usually sex rather than drugs. Maybe your Claudette was into that.'

'It had crossed my mind, but she'd need a well-placed pimp for that.'

'They exist, but as I say, I haven't seen any of it. We're not all that up-market as far as hotels go and the customers are pretty middle of the road.'

'Know anybody else I could try?'

'Oh yes, I think I know the man to see . . .'

Des left the hotel with slight reluctance. He'd got used to sitting in that anonymous lounge and, perversely, had felt quite at home. That's what they're about, hotels, making you feel at home, Des thought. And, somehow, being alone among strangers is kind of homely. Like there are no reminders. The grind of life suspended and you can lie back on your well-made bed, rootless and free.

Des smiled to himself and blinked up at the bright sky. Vera May was looking down at him from the fourth floor. It was strange sight, a memory glimpsed briefly, a life once touched ready to be filed away. He waved and then got in his car. A certain Harry Sharma awaited. *Yeh, Miranda, who the hell was she?*

*   *   *

There was something about the sun on the herb plants that made Vin think summer was on the wane. It didn't quite have the strength and its light was a paler yellow. An indication that he would have to harvest soon. He smiled. It was a good observation, a country instinct. But he also felt a sense of relief. At any time someone could stumble upon his secret patch. Worry was always with him when he went to the canal. For some time he'd been considering buying high-power lamps and growing weed in his loft, but the outdoor option was too alluring. Less quality, more fret, but it was his patch of back home in the concrete city. Vin opened up his bag of fertilizer and started scattering the white granules at the base of his plants. He didn't see the man leaning against a brick wall and rolling a joint for some time. Vin almost bumped into him before he turned suddenly and staggered back in shock.

'Jesus fuck, man!'

And then came the familiar snigger, the childlike smile and Scobie flicking at a curl on his forehead. 'It's the man from Del Monte,' he said.

Vin pulled himself together quickly. This was a serious situation. This was a man he would never want anywhere near one of his own operations. He put his hand in his pocket and fingered his knife.

'How the hell you fin dis place, man?'

'Saw you one time going down the cut and got curious.'

'You follow me?'

'Just watched where you went, the rest was easy. I mean, how could you miss this jungle?'

'Dis ain't nuttin to do wid you, Scobie.'

'What's it got to do with you, Vin? Anybody could've planted these . . . It's Waterways land.'

'You know dis is me lickle patch. It me business.'

Scobie finished rolling his spliff. 'Thought I'd try out the goods.' He lit up and set himself in the pose of a connoisseur. 'Mmm, a little coarse on the throat and weak as piss, I'd say.'

'Bugger off huh, Scobie.'

'Still, you've got quite a lot of flower heads, so I guess they'd have a fair buzz.'

'Come on, man, split.'

'Why don't we go fifty-fifty, eh? You never know in a place like this what might happen. Anyone could stumble on em and nick the lot, but for fifty-fifty, well, I could give some protection.'

Vin felt his spirits begin to sink to his knees. It was one hell of a shit situation and he could see nothing but hassle. Scobie would probably steal the lot, or just burn the crop for the fun of it. Whatever happened, he was sure Scobie would try to humiliate him. Humiliation – the word felt like a knife in his heart. Vin grabbed the handle of his own blade. He felt a sense of loathing, for himself and Scobie. But then something more dangerous entered his mind. This was his crop, his land; this was at the root of him. Vin pulled out his knife and lunged.

*   *   *

Harry didn't want to meet up in his hotel. This was a security guy who wore a leather blouson and a black turban. Harry was a bearded warrior Sikh, young and proud. He was also someone who believed in the age-old practice of tipping, so Des shifted another fifty quid of Bertha's dosh and hoped it would be worth it. They met at the Merchant Stores, a sort of up-market wine bar on

Broad Street. But there were no conventioneers or Japanese industrial heritage freaks around. A couple of suits were lingering long after their lunch break and that was it. Des lit up a fag and swirled the ice in his malt. It didn't seem so inviting as the time he'd given Rebecca the bad news. Harry had an alcopop (the arsehole); he dug his hands in his jacket and tapped relentlessly on the floor like life was busy and this dick was slowing him down. Des went into his spiel once more. He kept it brief and matter-of-fact, and hoped he'd out-cool the warrior.

'So it could be that these two got into some fuckery with a hotel punter.'

Harry eased up on the tapping and gave Des his attention. He had a lean, well-groomed face with wary, sharp eyes. Des thought he was probably black belt as well as black turban.

'Yeh, that's heavy business.'

'So the job now is to get hold of Gary Marlow.'

'Yeh.' Harry stared out of the big window of the Merchant Stores and watched a couple of women stride past. 'Well, you know, my hotel puts up a lot of celebs, you know, pop stars on the road, actors, and it's my job to keep an eye on such people, liaise with their minders and stuff.'

'Do you know this Gary then?'

'Sort of. I mean, I don't do any deals with clients. The hotel has to be strictly clean, but we do kind of indulge some of these celebs, you know, their little numbers. Then it's my job to keep it discreet and out of sight.'

'Of course, you wouldn't buy coke for a lead guitarist.'

'It'd be me out of a job, but I know the guy you mentioned.'

'Huh-uh.'

'Well, I say I know him, but I haven't met the guy, and didn't know nothing of the guy until he did a split.'

'Quite a relationship.'

'It was a week or so back. These guys were coming up to me, you know, minders and the like, and they kept asking me where the hell Gary was. You know, the dealer had gone and the punters were hungry. I was asked if I could supply.'

'Tricky.'

'I have a few connections. I went out and found someone else to do the dirty work, part of the service, and I heard then that this Gary Marlow had buggered off down the Smoke because of some fucked-up deal.'

'Was that all you heard?'

'Yeh.'

'Any idea were he lived?'

'Nah.'

'What about Claudette, ever hear about her?'

'Nah, but I guess I could ask round, you know, if it was . . .'

'Yeh, worth your while. You don't, of course, know who pimps for your snorting stars?'

'They don't need them, man. I just have to make sure the right groupies get in.'

'Huh, so what do you do with the ones that don't?'

'Wouldn't you like to know.'

Des left Harry tapping out time in the Merchant Stores. He didn't feel he'd made much progress but he was sure now that Gary Marlow was involved. One last call to make. The wonderful Fedora. It was only half a mile away so Des hoofed it through the city streets for a date with his DI.

It seemed that New Orleans had livened up that afternoon. The big eyes of Bogart were staring down at a party of eight: office people out on some kind of birthday binge. Wayne was actually busy and there was no Dick to be seen. Des cruised in and waved to Errol who lounged alone in the far corner.

'What's happening, Wayne?' he said. 'There's a third of a crowd in here.'

'Don't panic, Des, just the annual outing for the tax office.'

'Shame. Thought maybe it was the start of the big time.'

'I don't ever say it, Des, but fuck knows, the Fedora is and always will be a flop.'

Des got in a couple of whiskies and went and sat with DI Errol Wilson. The DI had a long line of peanuts set out on the table and was eating them one by one.

'You're late, man,' Errol said with a smile. 'You gotta know I'm too important now to be fucked around.'

'Wow.'

'I tell you, if I'd reached the last nut, I was off and out of it.'

'I'm a working man too, Errol.'

'Oh, I forgot. Another shit-heap place you've led me into.'

'This is the future, mate. It doesn't exist other than as an image of something that never was, an image that nobody cares about. It probably isn't even here. It's virtual, see, like we're probably sitting in the street now getting our shots of booze.'

'Jesus, Des, what the hell you on about?'

'Fuck knows. It's the Fedora, what it does to you.'

Des, feeling that his brain was beginning to speed after a long day's gabbing, quickly got down to business. And he felt smug enough doing it, even though the Gary Marlow lead wasn't his.

'Bleeding hell, ain't you the genius?' Errol put on an exaggerated show of admiration. 'I'm serious though, Des. That's good work.'

'I tell you, I'm off the bottom and moving up.'

'So how d'you do it?'

'Found something at Claudette's place that you guys had missed. Got in with the pros and found out more.'

'Yeh, well that is your advantage. That and the incompetence of some of our guys.'

'Could you check him for me, Errol, find out where his local pad is?'

'I reckon you deserve that.'

'So how are the flat feet doing?'

'Making our feet flatter. A lot of checking of pervs and so on. What you're digging up does seem to point to something closer to home.'

'Maybe too early to say.'

'Yeh, well I've got a bit of news that adds further spice to this case; it concerns your Bertha.'

'Huh-uh, I wondered when she might figure in the proceedings.'

'You know she was no angel in her younger days, a pro like her daughter?'

'Yeh.' Des sighed. He'd been trying to keep Bertha out of his mind. He'd been vaguely thinking he should keep out of her way. She knew his weakness.

'Well, man, I was talking to one of the old-timers down at the station. The guy remembers Bertha. Said she had a bit of a thing with Ross Constanza.'

'The name rings a bell.'

'You know him. Second-hand car dealer, backer of night clubs, escort agencies, cover jobs for piles of villainous fuck'ry.'

'Right.'

'There was some trouble, way back, involving another sleaze dealer – Paddy Conroy. Bertha got ditched and disappeared from the scene. The old-timer couldn't believe she'd surfaced again.'

'I can't see any connection with Claudette and now.'

'Mebbe not, man, but worth knowing, huh, what you're dealing with?'

'Yeh, guess so.'

'It would kinda make me want to watch my back.'

Des didn't say anything. He was thinking of the pink room and was wondering what else Bertha had to offer. He didn't want to admit it, but those thoughts turned him on.

10

It was the whiteness he saw first; a blanket of white, soft but overwhelming. And then it was the wet he became aware of, clammy skin-tight wet that made Des writhe. And after that, after the movement, he realized someone was pulling on his foot, tugging hard, attempting to drag him down. Des tried to look below, to see who it was who held him but it was pitch dark down there. 'Miranda or Bertha?' he muttered half conscious. 'Who the fuck is it with me?' Des continued to struggle, saw the whiteness even brighter above and then managed to prise open his eyes. He was totally drenched in sweat. Des pulled himself up onto an elbow and shook his head. 'Shit . . .' The room came into view. The cluttered, pale green room he'd spent many a sleepless or stupefied night in as he had lived, post-Miranda, with the big wallow. A shitty room he hated for all the memories it held. Des fumbled across the bedclothes and found himself a fag. He looked at the window. The sun was blazing away outside. Before the first traces of nicotine hit his hungry veins, the phone rang.

'So where have you been then, lover?'

'Jesus, Bertha, I've just woke up.'

'I've been up a while. Couldn't sleep. It may be hot outside, but my bleeding bed is cold.'

'I was pretty whacked last night,' Des lied, 'but I guess you were in my dreams.'

'Not good enough. After our night of passion I thought –'

'Yeh, I know, but let's –' Des felt a niggle of irritation. 'Let's, you know, let's try and keep a perspective. There's work too, yeh. There's your daughter to think about.'

A marked silence at the end of the phone. Des squirmed like a worm around the receiver. He cursed himself for being so ratty.

'Shouldn't have said that, should I? But then I guess it shows how complicated it gets.'

'I'm disappointed, Des.'

'Let's talk about it later, huh? I've been working and I've got news.'

Des quickly launched into a report about Gary Marlow, knowing that Bertha was far from happy but hoping he could distract her thoughts. Bertha reluctantly responded, distance and disappointment in her voice.

'You think he could've done it?'

'It's a possibility.'

'No one else involved?'

'Hard to say. He's done a bunk. Could be out of guilt, or fright.'

'Find out, Des.'

'That's what I'm doing.'

'And come and see me tonight.'

'Of course, I mean, I want to –'

Bertha had hung up on him. Des threw the phone back down on its cradle and realized he was still sweating. Swearing, he flung the covers off and began to scowl at the pale green walls. The phone rang again.

'Hi there, Sherlock, you up and at it yet?'

'Half asleep, sweating like a pig and pissed off, Errol.'

'Urgh, that makes me wanna put the phone down.'

'I don't think it's catching.'

'Better not be, man. It's bad enough as it is dealing with you low-life scum.'

'Thanks.'

'But some news, huh. I got an address for this Gary guy, for your use for today only, yeh?'

'That's good. I need something to sweeten up my client.'

'Poor you! We're also running a check down London to try to find out where he is. He's got a bit of form, man. A coupla drug busts, sounds like a user too, but no record of anything violent.'

'Thanks a lot, Errol. Give us the address then, eh, and I'll check you later.'

Des sat up on the bed. The sweat had finally chilled and he shivered. Maybe it was just enough to get him afloat. An old friend on the phone and something to do.

* * *

It was all too much for Jerry Coton. He stood on a suburban street a long way from home and felt as if – and maybe wished – he would spontaneously combust. He'd had a wasted journey to see someone he'd met in a pub about a one-off job. No someone, just a busy street in eighty-degree heat and no sign of a bus to haul him home. Jerry glared at the groaning traffic and tried to avoid the acrid fumes.

It had been a bad few days. The sickness was still with him, made worse by weed. He had a brain full of feathers and the world seemed like a cinema set he roamed with disbelief. He felt uncomfortable. Deep within him was a needle of fear, an insidious worry that kept him jittery. The anxiety had grown when Mary had a break-in. In the middle of the day when Jerry lay prone, spliffed and watching soap, someone had gone in and trashed her darkroom. He hadn't heard the intruders, but when he found out he almost collapsed at the thought of such malevolence coming so close. Mary was not sympathetic.

Jerry resolved to pull himself together, but the hours were long and the temptation great. He wiped sweat off his brow and struggled to breathe. A bus edged into sight. But would he be able to count the change for his fare?

Inside, it had to be one hundred and rising. There was no prospect of escape as the bus began its slow crawl through the suburbs. It wasn't long before Jerry got the shakes. An irritating twitch on his thigh to begin with, then a tic on his cheek and finally an awful sense that his head wasn't properly attached to his body. It really felt like his head was wobbling, that he'd suddenly lost the supportive aid of a spine. If held in his hands it felt all right, but left on its own, his head could've been a balloon flopping and straining to escape. Jerry began to think everyone was looking at him. Those hot faces that normally look anywhere but at another face, they were now slyly turning their eyes to watch the jelly-head wobble. He didn't know what to do. There was no escape. He found himself slipping down in the seat. He pushed his head against the window and wedged a hand under it. This stopped the wobbling, but then his head vibrated in synchronicity with the engine of the bus. Jerry sneaked a look at the snooping passengers. Why the fuck didn't they suffer? Such complacent faces like stupid sheep off to the slaughterhouse! He groaned and squeezed further into his caged space. Would the driver never stop?

He did stop. Jerry teetered onto the baking pavements of the city centre and resolved to walk the last few miles home. Out in the open, there was no more confinement to face. But the world still seemed out to harm him. Vertiginous buildings bending over and hurting his head. People blocking and bumping into him. People who sneered malevolently or mugged him with their eyes. Jerry kept his head down. He heard whining sounds, sounds like forks scraping plates or chalk on the blackboard. Dragging his legs along the hot pavements, he managed to haul himself away from the crowd and out to the quieter backstreets. Jerry still kept his head down. For some reason, he found himself distrusting gravity, fearing that if he looked up, he would fall from the ground and hurtle to the clouds.

The leafier suburbs closer to home offered a kind of relief. Fewer cars or people on the streets and the relative silence made things better for a while. But there seemed no way Jerry could get back to his normal old stuttering self. He soon began to suspect the silence and wondered why no one was about. Were all the people, the nerds, deliberately staying inside to avoid the wobble-headed loony? Or were they watching from behind those net curtains? Looking for signs of non-conformity or little misdemeanours they could shop him for? That really kept his head down but it didn't help much. There were so many trees in the streets – poplars, planes and limes – and they began to seem more threatening than the clouds. The limes were the worst. Horrible sweaty leaves covered in grime, and pallid flowers that looked like excreta from an alien planet. It was a lime tree that finally flipped him. Jerry just happened to glance up and there it was. A scrawny, grey monstrosity sat on a branch just above him. It had beady eyes and a white corrosive head. Jerry staggered to a halt and flopped against a privet bush. He tried to keep hold of himself, to enforce the voice of reason that said he was looking at a juvenile pigeon, but he couldn't. Suddenly, the whole tree began to sweat white flakes of ash or snow. His brain, his body, they just seemed to close down and he was paralysed. Only his eyes existed, floating, full of flakes of white and straining to see the bird's eye that drifted further away. He must've passed out then for a moment and when he awoke he found himself sitting on the ground, sweating, shaking and very scared. But Jerry got himself up with the bird still watching.

'F-F-Fuck you!' he cried, then staggered desperately, angrily the last few yards home.

*   *   *

A gun might have come in handy where Des was. Many of the thirty-year-old buildings looked close to collapse. On the far side of the road, all the flats and maisonettes that sat behind half-mature trees were grilled over with steel mesh. On the corner of a side street, a bunch of surly youths gave Des, the stranger, the once-over, like customs officers checking for illegal immigrants. Des merely sneered back and clenched his fists. It was proving a hard job to find Gary Marlow's pad. Half the road signs were missing or had been daubed illegible. Many of the little blocks of flats seemed to hide unmarked down alleyways. He had yet to see a friendly face he could ask.

The road he tramped along dipped down and he came to a bridge over a stream. Some joyriders had ditched a car into the grey, polluted waters. A hefty biker-type was directing a gang of kids to strip it of spare parts. Des took a left turn along a drive that led to another complex of boxes. As he walked, he almost dived into the stream as a ferocious Alsatian reared up above a garden fence and barked wildly. Finally, Des did find Gary's pad. Kicking his way through empty cans of lighter fuel, he ran up cold concrete steps and found the number of the door he'd been searching for. It had been kicked wide open.

Des entered cautiously. The heat of the day, though waning on the outside, was still intense within the flat. Smells of burnt debris mingled with those of piss and shit. There was no one in the place and not much left to make it a place at all. As he sneaked his way round, Des saw that the kitchen had lost its cabinets, cooker and fridge. The bathroom was minus its toilet and the bath had been smashed up. The living room was bare, bar a broken chair and a forlorn lampshade. Des began to sag. He wiped the sweat off his face and felt the frustrations rise within him. It seemed appropriate to kick the wall. He did and his foot went six inches in.

The last place to check was the bedroom. This was where the burning smell came from; the bed itself was a two-foot hole of charred stuffing. Des entered. Syringes and silver foil littered the floor. The cupboards here were built in but they too had been smashed. Clothes, magazines and other rubbish had spewed out around the bed to be kicked and trampled on. Des picked up a splintered piece of wood, sat on the bed and then began to prod around the rubbish. There was practically nothing there of significance. Male fashion mags and soft porn, broken CDs and slivers of mirror mingled with the mud-stained tiles and underwear. Des only found one thing, a torn triangular third of a black and white photograph, upon which Des could see a bare white bum.

The car was still in one piece when he got back to it. Des quickly clambered in and took off at speed. He opened his windows to let out the heat and the estate smells that lingered. Couldn't have been more than a few days, Des thought, since Gary skipped and his pad had already been stripped bare. Desperate times. Desperate place. Des pulled out the photo he'd found. It was on thick paper and there was a blurred edge to the print. The image itself was not quite sharp and a white smear at the side looked almost like a curtain. No professional piece of porn, Des thought, but then probably not a piece of anything. He threw the photo down and sighed.

'A hot, harrowing day in a fucking dustbin of the city and what do I get? A bleedin arsehole!'

Des allowed himself a smile and then he saw he was driving into familiar territory. Up ahead was the Vine. A large crowd of brethren were outside taking in the sun. As he drove past, Des thought he saw Vin St James, but he couldn't be sure. This guy had a bandaged head and his arm in a sling. Des carried on and it was then that he felt the tension grip him. He knew what it meant. He'd spent all day ignoring it. At the next crossroads he could go right and go home. A rather sour but a safe place. Alternatively, he could go left. There was a third-floor flat done out in pink. It was a risky place and bound to be fraught, but it had one hell of a bedroom.

11

The other side of someone. The moment when charm and affection slip away and a different face stares at you. One where configurations have subtly changed and sweet looks become nasty. Des was looking at a bloated, world-weary face with straw hair. He noted for the first time the sagging lines that left Bertha's lips and made her chin protrude. And he noted too the eyes, frosted over and hard.

'I've had a really shitty day,' Des said, trying to ignore the admonition in those eyes.

'You chose the job.'

Bertha sat stiffly on her maroon sofa and didn't exactly encourage Des to feel at home. He sat down anyway and tried to loll, thinking that Bertha's eyes were not just scolding but testing him too. This was power play. She wanted him squirming on the floor.

'Yeh,' Des drawled. 'Guess I was a naïve bugger to choose this line of work.'

'At least you're getting paid, well . . . by me.'

'True enough.' Des began to feel irritation rise within him. He dug out the torn scrap of photo. 'And this is the result of a hard day trawling through crap.'

'Uh huh, very informative. What is it?'

'An arse.'

'I can see that, but what's it mean?'

'Thought you might know that. I mean, you've been

around. It's possible it could belong to Claudette.'

Des half expected a blow from Bertha. She rounded on him, but then she turned up the cold control in her probing eyes. Words finally came out of a tight mouth.

'You are a cheap piece of shit, aren't you, Des? A piece of scum who thinks he's a big boy. Crap, you're just a tosser like most men, exploiting people's problems and grief.'

'I see –'

'Call yourself an investigator? A lost soul more like, looking for a mummy and a bit of cheap sex on the side.'

'Come on, Bertha, so I'm the one who's using you? No way –'

'You're doing all right, aren't you? You get my money, sleep in my bed – and then you treat me like dirt, bugger off, do your own thing as though I'm just a service provider.'

'You got me into bed. I didn't think it was such a good idea.'

'Oh, you were very reluctant.'

'I knew this would happen.'

'I want respect, Des. I need to trust you.'

'Trust? Well that's fine if it works both ways.'

'What's that supposed to mean?'

Des had to hand it to Bertha. Those unflinching eyes, not a sign of defrosting in them.

'What it means is that you haven't levelled with me. Past glories, Bertha, like living with Ross Constanza and having an affair with some other porn merchant.'

That one almost caused a crack in the ice. For a second, Bertha looked away. 'So that's it.'

'Well, come on, these guys are still around, in the same trade. For all I know, you and Claudette, you could still be connected.'

Bertha lowered her eyes and looked down at the Dralon seat. 'God, still paying for my past . . .'

It was quite a story. And a winning one too. Des, though feeling tetchy, skin still crawling with the germs and chemical detritus of a lost part of the city, forgot all his reservations about Bertha. Once more he saw those past glories in her face and not contemporary weariness and pain. Bertha had been a student once but, in a search for cash, had become drawn into the dodgy glamour world of escorts and stripping. It had been a laugh. Exciting to delve promiscuously into a world of ogling, uptight men who desperately wanted a turn-on. It was at that early stage that she met Ross. She got heavily into drugs and ended up whoring. Dark days followed, loss of self-respect, a youthful view of the future turned sour. Bertha said she thought she'd end up an ageing hooker.

'Lumbered with bleedin kids, stuck on the Social but still touting for trade, getting gormless drunk at weekends and bawling abuse at the night sky . . .'

Ross had left her to go bumming round the world. But then one day he came back and looked her up.

'He was oozing serious money and saying how he'd missed me madly. He took over my life. I was on a totally different level.'

That was when they started the escort and procuring agency. Bertha got off the game and organized it all. But Ross got into other things and started sleeping around. Bertha took a shine to Paddy Conroy and Claudette turned up in her womb.

'There was one hell of a bust-up. Ross beat the shit out of me and then he went after Paddy. There was a big fight at the King's Arms. One of Paddy's pals, Derek Cross, got killed. The law blamed it on Ross and he did five years for manslaughter.'

Des sat back on the sofa and thought about his own past. No CV to match that. Plenty of scrapes, bits of dealing, torrid affairs but nothing to equal that. He looked again at the lines on her face and wondered what events were responsible for which lines.

'So what happened after that?'

'A slow descent into oblivion. Paddy was scared off. I had Claudette and just had to scrape a living somehow. I got secretarial qualifications and have bored myself silly ever since.'

'Come on, you must've had a few affairs and the like.'

'Nothing much, nothing that stuck. I had my daughter and I did everything for her. For a long time it was enough, it more than compensated for the lonely nights and, you know, the frustration.'

'And now?'

'I guess I lost her when she went on the game, and now I've lost her for good.'

Des went with the eyes – thawed now, pools of brown melt-water – and put his arms around Bertha. 'I guess I've been a bastard.'

'Yeh, but maybe not as bad as some I know.'

'I dunno.'

'Well, you've been pretty clogged up with posh Miranda.'

'Shit, don't mention her.'

'Never look at the surface, eh. You've got to get in deep, right down to the muck, to pull out the best of gems.'

'The best of gems and the worst of nightmares.'

'Let's go delving, huh?'

'You mean into the pink?'

'I guess you are with me, on my side . . .'

'Yeh, guess I am.'

Bertha looked up to her pink paper flowers and smiled.

'No blame,' she said quietly, 'but also totally to blame. That's what experience is.'

*   *   *

Way out in the sprawl, Paddy Conroy had got himself shacked up in a part of the city Bertha had never been to before. A maze of des-res detached and semis in Shirley, solid investments for accountants and insurance men – conventional and desperately boring. What happens to people when they get old? Paddy used to be a cool guy. A hip Irish shark. Smoking dope with the rude boys, playing mixed up jazz and jigs on his mouth harp. Paddy was a laugh, a light-touch charmer who made things happen. Bertha turned her car right and went further into the bland lands of the city, wondering how a bright spark could end up there. She knew it was a risky venture but felt she couldn't wait any more. Maybe Des was pushing the boyfriend angle but Bertha was inclined to go with intuition. Ross, he was so much part of the scene, he would have to be involved somewhere. This was her hope; this was the chance she had to prepare for. She allowed herself a smile as she thought of Des still sleeping. She once again tried to reassure herself that it wasn't all planned.

Fuck, he already knew the outcome. Men just sucker themselves.

Paddy Conroy had a balding head and a big gut that pushed out of canvas slacks. A podgy face, almost unrecognizable, except for the bright smiling eyes that remained beneath a seriously wrinkled brow. Bertha was nervously greeted and reluctantly let in. She sat in the oyster and cream sitting room and tried to avoid the cold, fading-beauty looks of the blonde woman who offered tea. Paddy sat down opposite, leaning forwards, his arms on his knees and his hands restlessly intertwined.

'So are you married now, Paddy?'

'Just living together, Bee.'

'You look a hell of a lot different.'

'And you, we've all got the same incurable disease.'

102

'Yeh.' Bertha began to feel uncomfortable. She hadn't expected Paddy to be so uptight. 'Bit of a shock to see me, eh, and perhaps not a good time?'

'You should've rang.' Paddy looked behind him towards the kitchen and then lowered his voice. 'Cass, she's a bit . . . you know, she don't trust me with other women.'

'Well, you've still the old twinkle in your eye.'

The tea arrived and Cass stayed resolutely present. The situation depressed Bertha. The room, sparse, tidy and uncluttered. A restrained and gone-to-seed Paddy. A staid white suburb where you had to get in your car for a packet of fags. But she tried to make the most of it. She said she'd come into some money and was thinking of getting back into the business. There were rumours, she said, that Ross Constanza might be getting into trouble. A lie maybe, but she knew she need say little more. For Paddy, a less successful Paddy, had long sworn to get his revenge on the 'deformed little Eyetie'. She didn't mention Claudette's death, and Paddy showed no signs of knowing. It was a difficult subject and one Bertha couldn't raise in front of Cass. Who was the father, Ross or Paddy? The time when Claudette had grown in Bertha's womb was not one when such a question could easily be resolved. Ross was on his way to prison and didn't even consider the child; while Paddy, he went missing for a bit, and backed down on what could've been a territorial war. Some time later he did ask Bertha. 'Who knows, who cares?' she replied and was happy to keep it that way. But that wasn't the purpose of her visit. She had but two aims. Two seeds planted. Cass cleared up the tea things and took them away.

Paddy took his brief chance. 'I'm interested,' he said quietly, 'but don't ever call or come here again. I'll give you my office number and we'll arrange a time for a proper talk.'

'We should have a few drinks together, Paddy, in some old Irish dive and get nicely sozzled.'

'I can't talk like that now, and I'm not supposed to drink. I'm supposed to be a reformed man.'

Paddy whispered those last words. Bertha smiled widely and winked.

'You're missing something,' she said. 'Our age, it's second childhood time. We've done it all and now we can have fun.'

'Jesus, Bee, that sounds too naughty to me.'

'Well, Paddy Conroy, it could well be.'

* * *

How long can you make a cup of tea last? It is a serious question when you are down at rock bottom. Des McGinlay considered this as he sat in Kropotkin's Diner watching a scruffy dosser string out a cup of camomile tea. There could, Des thought, be a Buddhist art to it. Out of destitution, a kind of fruitful path to meditational ease. That, or a useful exercise in bloody-mindedness. Either way, the situation irked Des because he loathed the smell of the dosser and the tea. But then the whole café tended to have that effect on him. He liked the idea of anarchism but found most of its adherents obnoxious. Like Col, the guy behind the counter. It wasn't just the dayglo green brush that bisected his head, or the staples in his nose and the studs in his ears that bothered him, it was more that there was something strangely clinical and contrived about it all. A look-at-me sign on a clean face that had nothing to say. The dosser was the true anarchist. Des shrugged, took another swig of coffee and tried to focus his mind.

Kropotkin's Diner had a media resource centre above it. A place that hired out visual equipment and offered darkroom time for rent. It was a long shot, not much to go on, but Des felt that porno photos could be involved in Claudette's death. Or not. Des figured that maybe the bum shot could be the work of a freelancer, probably not professional but maybe wanting to be, the sort of person who might use the resource centre. Des had just had a chat with the co-ordinator and some of his views had been confirmed. A tentative approach, the guy had said, cheapish paper, but maybe knowing what they're doing. He'd also given out a few names of dubious types who might be up to peep-show work. So Des was almost pleased. A dead-end it might be, but for a while the momentum was being maintained. It needed to be. Thought had to be forestalled. Thinking would only lead on to Bertha and the hold she seemed to be getting on him. Strung up by money and sex. Caught on the rebound from Miranda. Bertha, she with the dangerous past. Des grinned uneasily at the dosser who was licking the last drops of tea from his spoon.

'The way it goes,' he soothed to himself, 'no strings and one-off.' It hardly sounded convincing.

12

'I didn't put the damn thing there!'

'Oh yes you bloody well did!

'No way!'

'You've got your head where your arse is sometimes, Liam!'

'Just don't blame me, woman!'

'Look at the poor kid. He's covered in it!'

'Shit, that's the doorbell now.'

Des groaned, took his hand off the buzzer and looked up at a cloudy sky. Maybe he should go back to taxi-driving? But then again, you still had to deal with people.

'Aren't you going to answer it then?'

'Probably that friggin loan shark.'

A child began bawling inside the house and then, perhaps in retaliation, Des heard the television being turned up. Footsteps clomped towards the door.

'Jesus, can't you all shut up – and turn that telly down!'

The door to the house was flung open and Des found himself looking at a skinny, dishevelled guy somewhere in his thirties. The man picked at his nose and gave Des a quizzical look.

'So who the fuck might you be then?' he asked.

'God almighty,' Des said with a smile. He put his hand in his pocket and brought out half a bottle of Paddy's booze.

'Well . . . to be sure, God is always welcome here.' Liam

Bell beckoned Des to come in. 'We're right good Catholics, you can tell by the horde of sprogs we got.'

The living room was like some kind of aftermath, a nuclear war or earthquake perhaps. The floor cluttered with toys and paper. Several chairs upturned, as were cups on a table where a large black puddle spread and dripped onto the floor. A number of kids were sprawled there too and on the rest of the furniture. Another one sat directly in front of the TV. In the middle of this, a woman stooped, trying to dab off some black substance from a small, bawling child. The whole scene gave Des a headache. Liam shrugged his bony shoulders and pursed his lips.

'Grand, ain't it?'

'I need to talk to you, about photography.'

'Ah, well . . .' Liam looked around at the mess. 'We'll go upstairs.'

Stumble up more like, thought Des as he followed Liam out of the mayhem and up a stairway piled with old newspapers, teddy bears and the odd box. They ended up in the main bedroom. Des slumped down onto a double bed and unscrewed the bottle of whiskey while Liam propped up the cot which butted against an overflowing wardrobe.

'Sort of pushed for space I'd say.' Des passed over the whiskey.

'Bloody council haven't come up with anything else yet.'

'So d'you do commissions then?'

'Depends what you've got in mind.'

It seemed as good a way in as any. Des told him he was a private investigator who needed some special kind of snaps for a client of his. The usual scenario. Husband cheating on wife, the wife reluctant to believe it and needing a juicy eye-opener to make it come true.

'You want porno peeping-tom shots?'

'You've got it. You've done it before, haven't you?'

Des pulled out the triangular piece of bum and waved it in the air. He got the whiskey back and Liam took the photo.

'This is not mine. It's a bit out of focus.'

'A reject shot, but you do this stuff, don't you?'

'The fuck I don't. Well, I've done some stuff with the wife like, but this isn't my scene.'

'No?'

'No, man. I mean, I'm interested . . . like you know, photography, it's an art form you can create with, make your own images. Tits and bums, that's just exploitational crap. Hold on a min –'

Liam handed back the photo, then knelt down and began to rummage under the bed. He eventually brought out a battered folder and slipped out a few black and white 10 x 8s.

'Like this is the stuff I'm into at the mo, low-light night shots.'

A fuzzy street-lamp shone in the top left-hand corner in one photo, all grain and blotted white with moth shapes. Below the light, pale girders loomed out of a dark background. Then Des saw a brick wall split dramatically in two by a thrusting shadow that pointed to a tattered boyband poster, their clean smirking faces made almost lunatic by the play of light. Then another shot, low-contrast grey light making barely discernible ripples on the surface of a canal. Dead-end night glimpses, images of insomnia.

'See what you mean.'

'I'm trying to explore the edge of things, man, you know, like where light begins to disappear and the photo is just a stop away from being no more.'

'Sounds profound, like photographing death or some-thing.'

'Yeh. Yeh, I hadn't thought of that.'

'With what I'm working on, it's not such a crazy idea.' Des passed over the whiskey again. 'So, if you don't do any hanky-panky stuff, you know someone who does, or have you heard of someone doing it?'

'Yeh . . .'

Liam was looking at his own photos, beginning to get lost in them.

'I mean, yeh, some time back,' he said. 'You meet like-minds down the resource centre and I was chatting to this bird one time and she mentioned she'd been asked to do dodgy stuff.'

'Now this is what I'm looking for, Liam.'

'Mary Holmes, a New Age sort of hippie-type. She lives on Ivor Road.'

Des left Liam squinting at his dark, sparse images thinking that maybe they were a kind of retreat for a harassed man. But he was also thinking of someone else whose eyes were like a shutter witnessing her last blink of light.

*   *   *

Mary Holmes had just got home from her part-time job at Kelly's bookshop. It was always a good time. Just after lunch with the house quiet and no more responsibilities for the day. She could easily spend an hour lounging on the sofa, maybe reading the paper, daydreaming or thinking about the things she had to do. She was considering her options then – a nice long bath, go up and see Jerry and spend an hour or so in bed, or perhaps a good session in the darkroom. She knew she needed to do the latter most. The burglary had almost knocked her back to square one. She had hardly anything left of her portfolio and had only just got the equipment functioning again. But it all felt a bit too much like work and she was still feeling uncomfortable with the violation of the burglary. She began to feel that she should leave that until later, much later, at a time when she'd felt she'd pleasured herself well. Mary stretched and moaned sensuously. There was no argument – a spliff, a bath and a large dollop of sex.

Downstairs, at the back of the house, someone was using a window as a mirror. He ran his hand over a frowning brow and then pushed his fingers into ochre hair, enjoying the thickness of it and the curls that rippled back over his head. Scobie was very proud of his hair. A lion's mane, virile and strong. He gave it one more tousle and began to move further round the house to the fire escape. It looked solid enough, though the rail seemed frail. Scobie noticed the open door on the first floor. This was the kind of job he enjoyed. A simple case of putting the shits up someone. And a woman at that, a blundering amateur who posed no threat. Scobie put on a casual smile and quickly made his way up the steps. He didn't hesitate at the kitchen door, strolled on through and pulled out a sharp knife as he did so. Mary seemed to find it hard to believe he was there. Scobie smiled, bowed his head a little and then walked over and cut the phone line. Mary only really registered his presence at that point and became paralysed with fear. But she had no time to react. Scobie came round the sofa and put the knife to her throat.

'So, darling, a bit surprised to see me, eh?'

'Wh-Who are you? What –?'

'I ain't here to answer questions, dear, only to ask them.'

'God . . . you can, you can take whatever there is, b-but there's not much, I've already been done.'

'Mmmm . . .'

Scobie suddenly lost his line of thought. He'd noticed Mary's supine body and a familiar feeling was beginning to surface. It wasn't supposed to. He had very strict orders from Ross. But he'd done something bad last time, really bad, and secretly knew that he'd enjoyed it too much. Scobie struggled to concentrate.

'I know all about you being done cos it was me what done it. We found the negs, darling, but we didn't find no prints.'

'What n-negs?'

Mary found herself utterly frozen. She seemed to have no sensations in her body other than a vague feeling that she needed a pee. She felt as if she was just a brain, a whirring, buzzing brain with all its circuitry in panic.

'Come on, you're well out of your depth. You don't know where I'm bleedin coming from?' Scobie widened his smile. 'But the fuck I'll tell you, darling, that I come from something bleedin bigger than you could imagine and we're dead unhappy with you. Straight answers, OK, darling, straight and clear or it's a shitty bin bag and a landfill site for you.'

'I don't . . .' Mary still couldn't think straight.

Things happened very quickly then. Scobie grabbed Mary's hair, moved round the sofa and began to wrench her up. Mary yelled in agony as she struggled to support her weight. The grinning face moved in close. 'Where're the bleedin prints?'

A fist suddenly thumped into Mary's face. There was a cracking sound and blood began to pour from her nose. She fell back onto the sofa, her ears ringing loudly, and she was conscious of the words deep down that she knew she had to bring up and out. As she fell back, Mary's skirt had swept up across her body and Scobie was suddenly looking at underwear. His next punch stalled, he found himself ogling and getting that feeling back again. Shit, he thought, what's the rush, why turn it down, what's Ross gonna know? He crouched and put his hands on bare knees. 'Well, darling?' he said.

Mary saw the change in his manner. She was shaking uncontrollably now and trying to keep the blood out of her mouth. Scobie's hand began to paw upwards, like a butcher's on a joint of meat.

'I don't have any prints,' Mary finally managed to blurt out. 'I gave them all to Claudette and that's the honest truth!'

'Did you now?'

Maybe it was the way he said the words, like he had stopped listening; or maybe it was those awful hands on her trembling flesh; but something snapped in Mary. With a shriek, she kicked Scobie in the chest and sent him tumbling backwards. Then she jumped up and ran, ran to the kitchen and stumbled through. She ran to the fire escape, hit the rail hard and then, Mary was suddenly flying, flying and falling like a swooping swift under blue sky . . .

*   *   *

Des should've been there, following leads, making progress; he could've arrived before Scobie; but Des actually ended up asleep in his car. It was the compensatory tipple of whiskey that did it – *for having endured a mind-numbing bout of family life*. The experience had brought back uneasy recollections. His own family years, splattered here and there with spurts of love and hate. One tipple led to another. One experience got generalized. All the houses in the street around him, all the streets multiplied – families sprawling for miles and miles, all cosy and self-contained, browsing drowsily and awesomely quiet. The thought comforted Des. He felt that at least he was out on the street, living in cracks and fissures where people were exposed and nothing was predictable.

One tipple leads to another. The bottle then becomes a

112

teat, a breast of comfort for one alone in an empty street where all windows point inwards. Families . . . Des thought of Bertha, her enticing bosom and experienced hands. And maybe why not? It was some sort of nestling place in the fissured world where the fate of hearts is a mere lottery. And then Des drifted down to dreams, crazy game-show dreams with 'real love' prizes. Des was a contestant, shabby and exposed, watched the world over by families, fast-food grazing, bored and forever unsatisfied.

13

Ivor Road on a sunny late afternoon. Kids out playing cricket in between the long lines of parked cars. Des drove exceedingly slowly, wary of darting youths and a fierce sun that splintered through over-arching trees. Sweat dribbled down his jaw and his mouth felt like fur. As he cautiously progressed, Des peered through the street clutter to check out house numbers. He needn't have bothered. The one he wanted was the one with the cop cars outside. Des parked and then let the sun warm his closed eyes. For a moment he could've been out on the coast resting from the optic sparkle of the waves. But it was only the briefest of moments where dusty plane trees had turned to tamarisk. Very soon his head was thumping. He knew he would have to open his eyes and confront more pain. As he got out of the car, the word 'Miranda' suddenly sounded in his mind and Des felt a surging hunger for flight.

There was quite a crowd outside Mary Holmes's house. Intrigued, excited, sad. Brown faces mostly, warmed by the sun and maybe the knowledge that it had not happened to them. Des eased his way through. There were a couple of cops by the gate; one had a scar that spliced his nose. Des hesitated but then caught sight of Errol emerging from the rear of the house. A confident smirk began to form. Des slipped under the barrier and smirked even harder at the cop who wore his nose with pride.

'What the hell d'you think you're doing?'

Des tried to lord it even more, feeling that there was some compensation for woe in being able to flaunt himself at the hard-faced cop.

'Just get me DI Wilson, will you?'

'Go fuck yourself.'

But Errol had already spotted Des and he came over. 'How come you're here, man?'

'To this door a lead has brought me.'

'Shit, you'd better come in.'

Des gave one final defiant smirk and then allowed himself to be ushered in where the big boys were.

Errol and Des stood in the overgrown back garden, the sun now lost behind a wall and the place busy with forensics.

'Yeh, the rail on the middle landing there just gave way and she fell bout fifteen feet. Might've survived but for the brick yard and the serrated chimney pot she clonked her head on.'

'Jesus . . .'

'Instant death.'

'So was it an accident or what?'

'Could've been, but there was blood on the sofa in her room and her phone line had been cut.'

'Jesus . . .'

'We've got a vague description of a guy hanging around, but nothing else as yet.'

'You say it happened a couple of hours ago. Jesus, I could've been here then.'

'Huh-uh, so why weren't you?'

'Fell asleep on the job.'

Des had almost been wondering what the job was. Farting around with nothing but a scrap of a photo and Claudette's death seeming like ancient history. But this development, this was a shock; it was a justification he didn't want.

'Come on then, Des, explain your angle.'

'Jesus . . .' Des sighed and felt the ache in his head even more.

'That's the fourth time you've said that, man. Could you, you know, try another word?'

'Daytime drinking, Errol, it's a . . .' Des stopped himself saying 'killer' and then got out his scrap of photo.

'It's just an arse, I know, but I found this at Gary's wrecked pad and thought maybe that him and Claudette could've been into porn or blackmail, so I was checking out possible snapshotters and this woman's name comes up.'

'Jesus . . .'

'Errol!'

'No, what I mean, this woman had her darkroom done over a while back, had a lot of stuff nicked. One of the DCs remembers coming here, said it was a nasty break-in, a lot of damage and all of her neg boxes gone.'

'Sod it, Errol, is this fitting into place? Is it me or what?'

'It could still be a coincidence, but I reckon we should get together on this quick.'

'Who found the body?'

'A guy called Jerry Coton. Lives in the top flat. He was cut up pretty rough and couldn't tell us much. Looked pretty stoned to me.'

'Yeh, who wouldn't want to be?'

'With that guy it's probably permanent.'

'Seems sane enough to me.'

'You're not sounding too good, Des.' Errol narrowed his eyes and gave Des a once-over. 'I mean, are you in control of this situation? How are you handling Bertha?'

'I don't reckon I know, Errol. Whatever happens is about as far as it goes.'

*   *   *

116

There was a picture of Mount Everest next to the Cute of the Month. That was Ross for you, a cute cunt and a big tit of a mountain. Of course, Ross would put it in a more 'refined' way: 'A peak of achievement in the glamour business.' Scobie secretly scowled. What a tosser! The guy was just a piece of gutter shit like the rest of us. Just because he read a dictionary once doesn't change fuck all. It's only a line of guff anyway for the men in suits but he seems to think he can pull the same shit with everyone.

'Are you listening to me, Scobie?'

'Sure.'

'I am really trying to get it into your thick skull that I am not pleased.'

'I got it the first time.'

'I don't know if you did. Two-inch thick – that or you're just pretending to be dim.'

'Come on –'

'No, you – Jesus, think I'll get Gus to bring the drill in – look, final last time. I did not tell you to fuck Claudette, I told you she needed to go away permanently.'

'So what's it matter?'

'What's it matter? It matters because they've got your genetic fingerprint. That means they've got you one hundred plus per cent for doing Claudette and that means they've most likely got me.'

'They don't know anything.'

'Right. Maybe. So then what happens? I tell you to put the shits up this photographer bitch and she ends up dead, and no doubt screwed too. What's the matter? Are you not getting any or something? Are you losing touch with reality?'

'No! The fuck no! I never touched her! She was the nutty one. One minute rigid as a rock, the next dashing off like a mad animal. There was nothing the fuck I could do about it.'

117

'It's an almighty mess, Scobie, it really is. Two deaths will mean four times the effort by the police and that means heat for me and diarrhoea for some of my clients!'

Words, his bleeding mouth's got the runs! What an arsehole! Scobie thought. The cops will never make a connection anyway. A tart gets bumped off and a drugged up hippie falls off a fire escape; big bloody deal. Scobie continued to seethe quietly at the bollocking his boss was laying out. He stared at the missing finger and began to imagine slicing off the rest of them. The joke was that Ross lost his finger while touching up a Nepalese whore who had a cunt like a clam. The truth was supposed to be that a rabid dog did the business, which explained why Ross himself was a nutter and liable to do nasty things. But Scobie had other ideas. Years of wanking had worn it down, that was one. Another? The guy was talking so much one time that he bit it off himself without even knowing it.

*　　*　　*

No matter how many tart-ups it had, the Crown always ended up looking like a dive. The landlord, a West Indian old-timer, didn't really give two shits for what the place looked like. 'Back-a-yard dem have bleedin tin hut wid tea chest fi sit pon. A pub, it a drinkin place. Who care what it look like?' he'd say. So Reuben just left the fingermarks and beer stains alone. Posters of past events became permanent, as did the felt-tip exhortations to Jah, long forgotten posses and the bloodclaat pros from down the road. Only the bottles of booze and the well-worn bar sparkled, as did the big screen satellite TV that flooded the ceiling blue and silver. Jerry and Frederick eased into a corner away from the old men who pumped fruit machines and slapped their way through endless dominoes.

Frederick set the tone of the night by lining them both up with a pint of bitter and a large white rum. The big screen that hung safely from the ceiling was showing some Stateside boxing match. Nobody seemed bothered with it; all the intercourse of noise was rooted to the floor.

'You feelin a bit better now, man?'

'I d-don't know . . .'

'Jus let it ride, man. Nuttin else much you can do but get piss and let it ride.'

Jerry nodded and lit up a fresh fag from the butt of his old one. His face was grey and sweat-flecked, his lips were trembling and he didn't dare to try to keep his fingers still. But though he found it hard to utter more than two words at a go, he was pleased that Frederick had taken him in tow. Earlier, at the Lime Tree, he had sat alone looking down into a deep pit where Mary lay bloody and smashed. He couldn't see anything else, couldn't envisage ever closing his eyes and was scared to try to think or feel. But old grey Frederick had come along with soothing words and a fatherly arm to guide him into oblivion. The Crown was the third pub of the night.

The movement of booze began to increase. The bitters sank to halves but the rums began to rise in their glasses. The pub had become more crowded and the noise of revelry flooded in. Frederick's tales of female conquests soon got lost in the blather. Jerry's eyes began to glaze and stare blankly at other guys cackling in competition with each other. Then his eyes drifted to the screen in the sky and the heavy sparring that took place there. It wasn't long before Jerry was in there with the punches, as if that was a way to exorcize his pain. Willing on thuds to the body and wincing at the slow-mo crunch of punches replayed. The whole situation seemed like a big spar. All the guys in the bar were fighting with words and gestures. The stylized slap of a domino was a provocation to war. Everyone was getting frigging worked up; the whole world was at each other's throats, dancing up and down with the rituals of the fight. Jerry felt like standing up and getting into a boxing pose.

'What's your problem, huh? Let me sock you with this shit! Mary's dead, you bastard, her skull's all smashed in!' he wanted to shout. But Jerry remained a pale-faced mute, a sad case in a bar of black revelry. Frederick clamped a large hand on Jerry's shoulder and pointed across the bar.

'It a Friday night. The girls dem a tekkin break from work.'

There was Ida, Sandy and there was Colette. The three women squeezed around Jerry and Frederick and suddenly the atmosphere changed. Well-cushioned thighs and brazen boobs pushed out and the raucous chat that had previously jarred was dispelled to the far reaches of the room. Frederick did the intros as he sneakily rolled a spliff on his knees.

'Social workers of the world, ennit, sisters?'

'Too right, Fred,' the big-shouldered Ida replied. 'There ain't a man's problems we don't fix.'

'Fuck the prisons, eh, jus gi em lots a pussy.'

'Yeh, well we ain't working at the mo, Fred, so leave it out, eh.'

'Yeh, you is right, sis.'

'So how's it goin with you, old man? How's the weary bones an that dreaded arthritis?'

'No way you shoulda mention dat. It like the weather, Ida, which in dis country is none at all good. Why you tink me a spliff up all the time?'

'Huh, that's just an excuse to get high and you know it. You wanna get into training, old man. That's what we do, ain't it, Sandy?'

Ida raised her arm to show off her biceps. She nudged Sandy as she did so.

120

'Leave off, Ida!'

'Blimey!' Ida turned back to Frederick. 'She had a real slimebag earlier on. We had to help her out. Jesus, you need to be fit.'

'Well you know what happen to Claudette.'

'Yeh. But it forgettin time now, ain't it? Time for fun, eh?'

'Too, too right.'

As Ida spoke, Jerry found himself looking at her nut-brown hands and the eight silver rings that adorned them. One had a skull on it. Jerry couldn't stop staring and suddenly felt his stomach churn. The sight of Mary's bloody head came looming. And then another hand reached out and touched Jerry's. It belonged to Colette, the one with the ginger curls.

'You all right?'

'J-Just about.'

'You feelin sick?'

'B-Badly.'

Colette pouted her lips and frowned. 'Now I'm here it ain't allowed.'

She smiled, shoved a fag in Jerry's mouth and suddenly the death's head receded. The flow of drinks increased as the girls began to blow hard-earned money. The laughter grew too, the girls taking the piss out of punters, talking telly and movies and most of all weighing the options of where they'd most like to be – Spain, Greece, LA, Orlando – it looked like Florida would win hands down.

'Stop dis dreamin!' Frederick shouted. 'The night it a young, the pub a closin an we should go party elsewhere.'

'Why not your yard, Fred?' Ida bawled.

'Oh no, me gotta much better idea.'

It was the end house of a condemned row. Looking out of a side window, all Jerry could see were dark humps of earth and brick rubble. The broken terrain seemed to last for ever, only ceasing, it seemed, at far-off lights in some other part of the city. The window was in the hall, a place a few precious decibels quieter than the rest of the blues party, where rap and reggae thundered. Heavy bass pounded into the walls and foundations, and then went off into the bowels of the earth. Jerry could see the house being prematurely demolished by the end of the night.

'Women dem a bitches, man. Dem play up like queens an mek man pay.'

'Ugh?'

Jerry was propping up a wall in the hall with a Red Stripe and a solid vibration up his spine. This guy Wishbone was talking. He was a kind of travelling salesman with a big bag full of dope, chocolate bars and overpriced fags.

'We the hunters man, an women, dey is creation, ennit? Pickneys an dumplins an sweet-scented fannies, right?'

'Er . . . right.'

'Right, an we out in the bleedin jungle gettin cut up and fuck up an strung way out, an all we friggin want, man, when we get back fi yard is a lickle bit a sweet –' Wishbone rubbed his fingers under Jerry's nose.

'Yeh, r-right . . .'

'Right, an do we get it? No fuckin way, man, less we kiss dem friggin feet firs!'

Jerry didn't know what the guy was on about or how come he was talking of sweet-scented fannies. Frederick had drifted off some time ago to rub-a-dub with the off-duty whores. He could see them grooving and soothing away the sweat of their labour with crackling bush and the rhythms of Africa. Maybe Frederick had said to the guys that Jerry was mourning or maybe it was his sad drooling eyes that Wishbone noticed as Jerry watched tight pants throb and hanging cleavages drip with sweat.

'But me don't tek none a dat now. Me mek sure me skirt a one who know me is the boss!'

Wishbone showed a gold tooth and then pushed a gold knuckle up towards Jerry's eyes. All he could do was grin. Copious amounts of dope and pummelling sounds had moulded him into a kind of fluid oblivion, a throbbing organism that just was, whatever went on around him. And that was good because the pain had gone. There was nothing but the numb beat, the uncomplicated pulse that went on and on.

14

The Mirpur Gardens wasn't exactly teeming with life. Only four others, two couples, sat up front by the plate glass window, their faces washed green by the restaurant sign. Within the rest of the room, surrounded by the gold-embossed flock of rose and vine, there was just one other person. Des McGinlay mopped up the last of his balti with a cold remnant of naan. The tables were covered with plum-coloured cloths and had sheets of glass on top. In the reflection of one, Des could see the cold cabinet with its trays of sweets and the disembodied, upside-down head of Zafeer. A disconcerting view that seemed to sum up how uncomfortable he felt. Sweat dappled his brow, a brow that felt taut as though ratcheted from behind. And the floral walls, they twitched and swirled in the corners of his tired eyes. Des gripped the edges of the table. The room, dimly lit, suddenly seemed to elongate and Zafeer, eyes almost closed, appeared twenty yards away, a shrivelled nut of a head bathed in the green neon glow. Des knew he had to move. He eased his way over to the counter. He paid the bill, fumblingly, cash clattering on glass, with Zafeer's bleary eyes looking out into the night for mathematical inspiration. It was a transaction of sorts, though the details seemed arbitrary. Des didn't mind; a hollow 'Cheers' and he was out into the cool night air.

It was what he needed, the air and the exercise. Back on

the move, eyes alert, on the lookout for Jerry Coton. He crossed Stoney Lane and entered the terraced streets, all yellow glare, deep shadow and covered windows hinting secrets. A taxi prowled past him looking for its fare. Then a pair of black ghost forms appeared. Purdah robes. Wary, they hugged the house walls and then scurried past Des. He caught the merest flicker of a furtive eye. Further on, Des had the feeling he was being followed, but there was no one to see. He shrugged. Just bad feelings on his tail. In that yard behind the wall, a death that should've been avoided. Over in the shop doorway, fear pretending to check out the small ads. And further back, in deeper cover, Miranda was doggedly clinging on. He gritted his teeth. Nothing much else could be done. It was a test of nerve.

Friday night and there was no Stevie Kitson down at the Lime Tree. This night seemed to attract mostly black clientele so Des didn't feel especially hopeful. Still, he pushed his way through the throng and wondered whether a drink would dispel the night creatures that followed him. He decided it would and ordered a large whisky. As he did so, he caught Eileen's eye and beckoned her over. It being pay cheque night, it was a while before Eileen came. Des surveyed the bar. There were few faces he recognized.

'Can't talk long, Des, what can I do for you?'

'Sorry, Eileen, just a quick thing. You seen Jerry Coton here tonight?'

'The tall guy who stutters?'

'Yeh, guess that's him.'

'Surely, he was here earlier on, but then went off with Frederick.'

'Old grey Frederick?'

'Huh-uh.'

'No idea where?'

'I think Frederick sometimes goes down the George.'

'Right.'

Des downed his whisky in one go. Then he felt a little something give him a tug. *Big wallow here. See all those smiling faces, that warm amber glow? How about, you know, another little shot before you think to leave?* Des stood up abruptly. 'No way,' he muttered under his breath. 'No way I fall for that again.' And he made his way through the crowd.

So it was once more out into the city streets where bad vibes prowled like ghosts in black. He went up a street of shuttered shops, all riot and ram-raider proof, and then turned the corner at the Dodyal Sweet House where bullet holes could still be seen in the concrete wall. He kept his head well down. Eyes on automatic de-select. If you don't see the shit, the world looks better. He didn't even look into the window of the all-night taxi office where grey-faced drivers kicked heels, chewed fat and went goggle-eyed in front of the TV box. Being this withdrawn, Des didn't see the guy coming round the corner. He couldn't stop his shoulder sending Vin St James flying.

'Jesus fuck, man!' Vin had landed on his backside. He angrily glared up at Des. 'It you! You the bleeda who sock me before. You the bastard who los me bes blade!'

'Sorry, man. Shit, let me help you up.'

'Don't you dare touch me, man!'

'You look like you need help. I mean, what happened, Vin?'

Vin was certainly struggling to get to the vertical. His left arm was in a sling and there seemed to be something wrong with one of his legs. He managed to get his weight on his good arm but then struggled to get his feet to move.

'Shit!' he gasped.

Des moved over, grabbed him under the armpits and pulled Vin up like a pillow. But he didn't get any thanks, merely a suspicious, surly look as Vin dusted himself down. Des noticed a set of stitches right across his brow.

'So what happened then, eh?'

'It ent nuttin feh you to know bout.'

'Come on, you know my interest. I'm still working for Bertha.'

Vin looked up and down the street. His shoulders seemed droopier than before and his cheeks more hollow. The guy had aged a lot in a week.

'Yeh, what the fuck,' Vin muttered.

'Did you get clobbered because of Claudette?'

'You t'ink me s'pose fi know dat?' The shoulders drooped more. 'Yeh, man, it probably was. Look, man, you put it togedda. Me go an see Ross Constanza, ask im if he know anytin bout what Claudette she up to. Im don't know. Few day later, Scobie turn up on me plot an me end up in a hospital wid me whole crop a trash.'

'Scobie?'

'Wha? You mean you don't know im?' Vin kissed his teeth. 'Scobie im Ross bad bwoy, im muscle. Man, me pull firs an im still get me.'

'I'm really sorry, Vin, but, you know, why would this Ross guy know anything?'

'Come on, you ain't that dumb, or is you jus playin the fool?'

'Hey –'

'Look, Ross im run girl too, at the posh end a the market. Me jus thought she might a gone to im feh extra dough. Turn out she was fuckin roun wid some other guy, but dat don't bother Ross. You ain't s'pose to question Ross.'

'You got any proof?'

'Man, me know nuttin right, cept me a fuck up bad an feelin pressure.'

'Well, thanks for the info anyway.'

'Don't t'ank me, man, cos it could be a curse.' Vin suddenly turned a shifty eye up and straight into Des's gaze. 'Scobie, the rat, im coulda come after you!'

A half-hearted laugh came out of Vin's mouth as he turned and limped away. Des leaned back against a wall. For a moment he was encouraged by what he'd heard about Ross Constanza. Another connection, another snippet of information that made the case move. But then he sighed loudly. 'Just another sordid little fix really,' he muttered to himself. 'So why am I roaming the streets?' Des set off once again for the George. 'Could it be because I don't want to go back to Bertha?'

The George Inn was considerably quieter than the Lime Tree. This was a Sikh-run pub and was known to be stricter in adhering to the rules. The clientele, therefore, were perhaps a bit more respectable. That, or they were serious drinkers unconcerned with pick-ups or partying. Des got himself half a bitter. He asked at the bar about Frederick but got the same story that he'd been and gone. He found a fairly quiet corner and slumped down. The temptation was to start picking over the case, and that would probably have happened, if a woman hadn't stared him out of his thoughts. She wouldn't stop looking, a ginger-haired mixed-race woman with mocking eyes and the prominent thighs of a girl in the trade. Des began to get shifty. Her face was familiar.

'You clocked it yet?'

'I'm working on it.'

'Could be a delicate matter, certainly embarrassing.'

'That's probably why I've forgot.'

'Think of precious jewels.'

'Rubies?'

'Better than that.'

'Diamonds?'

'No, this has a sea connection.'

'Oh no . . .'

It was the kind of situation that might have got Des

running, but there was something about Pearl that made him smile.

'I'm kind of surprised you remembered. One limp john must look like any other,' he said.

'You didn't come over as any john. You didn't even seem like a john, more like a guy who was having a bad time. A bit like now, huh?'

'Very perceptive.'

'It's useful to know how to size a guy up.'

'In one minute flat?'

'Often that's all the time there is.'

Des found himself beginning to relax. It was weird, her just sitting there and latching onto him, but there seemed no angles, no shit to be stirred. Is this friendliness, Des thought, that I am warming to?

'Do you normally do this? I mean, talk to ex-clients?' he asked. 'I guess this is your time off.'

'Too right it is. I come here for some peace and quiet. And you? Well you, I guess, aren't really an ex-client. I kind of respect a guy who isn't into cold sex.'

'Yeh?' Des wondered whether he was blushing. 'Well, it's nice to meet you, Pearl.'

'You too, mister.'

They both shook hands and Des suddenly thought of the sea and of a beach of yellow sand yet to be visited.

15

Old grey Frederick lived on the second floor of a converted Victorian house. A housing association job, Des could tell. He stood on the porch on a bright sunny morning and rang the relevant bell. It was almost a good mood day. He'd stayed away from Bertha. And there was a new spirit to warm up his weary heart. They hadn't stayed chatting for long, and it was just routine stuff about living in the city, but Des had actually made a date with Pearl. OK, so she was a pro and had a nasty pimp hanging around. She wasn't exactly a good catch, but for Des the date seemed like an achievement in the aftermath of Miranda and the deal he had with Bertha. He rang the bell again. Nine o'clock. It was disgustingly early he knew, but this was a good mood day and there was a big case to work on. 'Put it there,' Des said to a scruffy cat that came out of the shrubbery. He held out his hand. The cat sniffed it but then moved on to wait by the front door. 'You want him too, huh?'

The old guy did eventually come down and open the door. A black face, sallow and bereft of shine, Frederick peered out at the sunlight and groaned.

'Err . . . wha the fuck is it, man?'

'Your cat's hungry, Frederick.'

'Huh, neva nuttin else.' A red eye prised itself a little further open. 'Who the fuck are you, man, and why the fuck you wekin me up at dis lunatic hour?'

Des almost felt like launching into some kind of Jehovah spiel and taking the piss, but he managed to keep in a work mode.

'Yeh, sorry about this, but, well actually I want to see Jerry.'

'How'd you fin me, man, an im for dat matter?'

'I'm local, Frederick. I know who to ask.'

'Yeh . . . well, man. Jerry, im stone cold out, got block up to im eyeball las night cos im woman got kill.'

'I know, that's why I'm here.'

Frederick opened the door a little wider. Des saw a white shirt half stuffed into jogging pants. He also saw unshaven white fuzz on Frederick's jaw and thought then of Wayne, wondering whether he should get a match out and strike up for his first fag of the day.

'Well, man, me guess you can try an wek Jerry up if you want, but it'll prob'ly tek all day.'

Frederick turned towards the stairs, the cat at his ankles and Des following behind.

It could almost have been that Jerry Coton had joined Mary Holmes in the garden of rest. He lay on his back on the bed, white and totally immobile. His mouth resembled the last gasp of a fish drowned in air. Des did light up his first fag of the day and pondered the arts of resurrection. His first impulse was to want to shave off Jerry's straggly beard and comb his knotted hair as if he was an undertaker out to groom a corpse. But the sun was shining and urgent in his heart and Des was impatient to get on. Frederick muttered, 'What the fuck?' as Des got out the ice-cube tray and returned to the laid-out Jerry. A cube for each of the eyes, several slotted in the mouth and then the rest piled on a hardly moving chest. Des squeezed Jerry's nose and waited. Like a train approaching in the distance, a few vibrations began in Jerry's body, a few twitches and stifled snorts and then a more distinct and continuous writhing until Jerry jolted upright, spat out water and coughed raucously.

'Welcome back . . .'

'Wha –?'

'To the land of the living, man.'

Bloodshot eyes glanced briefly at Des in incomprehension before the coughing fit resumed. Des knew he was only halfway there.

The cornmeal porridge sitting before Jerry Coton looked more like an oral excretion than breakfast food. Des concentrated on plying coffee. It was the third top-up and still Jerry hadn't spoken a word. His elbows were pinioned to the table while the rest of him shivered, his red eyes staring implacably at a sugar bowl and the brown coffee stains that marred its contents.

'Come on now, man. Drink this up, you're getting there, you're nearly with us.'

But it was the best part of half an hour before the white face became tinged with colour and blurred eyes began to roam around the room.

'Sh . . . sh . . . sh-shit.'

'Yeh, right. Short, but I guess profound.'

'W-Where a-am I?'

Frederick moved over from propping up the cooker and put his big face close to Jerry's. 'My yard, man, you rememba? You got so friggin piss up las night me had to practic'ly carry you home.'

'Yeh . . . F-Frederick.'

'Dat's it, an dere's dis guy here, an investigator, im want to talk to you, man.'

It was a strain on Des's patience but eventually Jerry did fully join the world again, a world of sunshine outside and blackness within. He gradually began to tell Des of how

132

keen he'd been on Mary, of how their relationship had been 'sort of crazy' but good. It was a stuttering and half-garbled account with Jerry's eyes fretting all around the room.

'The really sh-shit th-thing . . .'

His words got stuck for a long time on that one but eventually Des got it sussed out. The really shit thing was that Jerry was in the house at the time of the attack. It was lunchtime and he was still in bed, half-stoned, half-asleep dreams swirling around his head. He sort of heard some noises but they never got through the reveries he indulged in. It was probably an hour later when Jerry crawled out of bed, went squinting to the fire escape and lit up his first fag.

'Shit, I always f-feel q-queasy on the f-fire escape, b-but I went d-down expecting Mary to c-come out of the kitchen s-smiling. And then I saw the b-broken rail and I l-looked d-down –'

'That must've been really bad.'

'I – I almost f-fell myself . . . wish I had.'

'Wouldn't have helped, Jerry. Just more tragedy.'

'God, I sh-should've b-been awake! I c-could've helped her!'

'You still can, Jerry, that's the thing, and you're going to do it. There must be something you know that can help finger the guy who did it.'

The coffee count was getting into double figures. Frederick had to nip out to replenish the fags. Half a slice of toast got nibbled away. Des explained his interest in the case and began to outline some of the things he'd found out. This seemed to help Jerry. A story to focus on. Actions that aimed for redemption. A firmer gaze entered his eyes and his shaking finally ceased. Des told him about the scrap of a photo he'd found and the talk that Mary had done a dodgy job. The comprehension within Jerry then became almost acute. Sharp eyes focused on Des.

'I – I've s-seen those photos!'

'You have?'

'Some old g-geezer having it off with a p-pro, d-doggy style.'

'You recognize them?'

'N-No, b-but, yeh I remember n-now. It was C-Claudette. M-Mary said she met her down the L-Lime.'

'And the guy?'

'I think I've still g-got a couple of her prints. She showed them m-me at m-my flat and they j-just g-got shoved somewhere.'

'Jerry – you can do something, and right now. Get your coat, for fuck's sake!'

The sunshine was still glorious but for Jerry it must have been insulting. He cowered in the corner of the car as Des set off for Ivor Road. There was no conversation and Des tried not to force it. He reckoned he knew about loss, not as bad, but something of what Jerry was going through. In five minutes Des was back under the trees, watching out for tennis balls and avoiding wobbly bikes. The cops still had the house cordoned off, though there was no one on guard. Des and Jerry slipped under the tape, unlocked the front door and went up darkened stairs.

'G-Guess I'd've had t-to c-come back today anyway.'

'The cops'll want to give you the third degree.'

'S'pose I could be a s-suspect.'

'Well, I wouldn't rule you out.'

'Thanks . . .'

The flat was sparsely furnished, though there was clutter enough at the edges of the rooms with books and magazines precariously piled. Jerry vaguely stared at them.

'I d-dunno . . .'

'You've got to find them, Jerry. They could be crucial.'

'Er, I w-was on the sofa and . . .'

With fidgety fingers, Jerry began to turn over the books and magazines on one particular pile.

'There was this other f-funny scene t-too.'

'Yeh?'

'M-Mary, she had a one-night stand with this g-guy who k-kept asking if she t-took dirty p-pictures.'

'You know who he was?'

'Can't remember, b-but he had a f-finger missing from one hand.'

'Won't be many guys like that.'

Jerry stopped searching for a moment. 'I feel f-funny, you know, about out there.'

Des followed the movement of his head. Through a door, he could see the kitchen and the fire escape beyond.

'Perhaps you should go back to Frederick later.'

'W-Wait, g-got it, this is the stuff!'

Des sat in silence looking at the two photos for a long time. It could be, he thought, that these were the cause of two murders. Two lousy shots of a guy indulging in whim or fantasy. Des didn't think they were particularly shocking, even though he recognized the faces. Dirty thoughts made real, dirty thoughts everyone has. But such is hypocrisy. Dirt found out is crime. It's crime that leads to greater crime which makes the dirt more guilt-ridden and cloaked in secrecy. He suddenly remembered his own stupidity, the red balloon madness when he went hunger-driven into the night. Des sighed. Well at least he'd put a face to the arse he'd been chasing.

'Y-You know who the g-guy is?'

'Sure, don't you?'

'N-No.'

'God, man, don't you read the papers?'

'T-Too right I d-don't.'

'This lunging stag here, Jerry, this rutting prick is none other than Sir Martin Wainwright.'

'Er, think I've heard the n-name.'

'Jesus! The guy's a bigwig businessman: car components, property development and all that shit. But he's high profile, this guy, spends his pocket money pushing for withdrawal from Europe and true independence for our beloved nation. His friggin face is never out of the papers.'

'Oh f-fuck . . .'

'Look, I'm gonna have to have these, yeh? This is important stuff, could get Claudette's and Mary's killer.'

But Jerry Coton seemed to have stopped listening. He dismissed the photos with a wave of his hand and slumped down onto the sofa. He gave the far wall of the room a venomous glare. Des slipped the photos beneath his shirt and made ready to leave.

'Don't tell anybody, huh? You don't know anything about them. These snaps, they attract death as surely as death attracts vultures.'

Jerry continued staring at the wall.

'You OK there?'

'God, I w-wish I c-could kill the bastard!'

*   *   *

Jerry took to the streets. It wasn't as if he wanted to be there, but home had lost its secure veneer, home had split open and left brains on the floor. He had no trouble walking away until he realized that the streets might be equally risky. Snooping eyes and damned pigeons. Panic whiteouts beneath dripping trees. But as he walked briskly on, he knew he would probably be immune. All that aching within, all that nausea, it brought a compulsion strong enough to resist spooky streets and lamp posts looming like sinister birds. He headed for the emptier places of the city, away from shops, cluttered stalls and the claustrophobia of suburbia. Like an animal in flight, Jerry

136

went for wasteground and the empty acres of expressways where no one walked and people sped past, anonymous as flies. He found himself on Camp Hill. A six-lane highway that swept down through brick factories and onwards to glittering office towers. Jerry stopped and stared.

'Nothing to d-do with m-me . . .'

He felt completely alone then. The moving machines became almost invisible, a blur of sound, a background drone within the morphology of the landscape. He was on the edge of a cliff looking down at the scenery. Human structures had become weird geology. The city was a plateau of rutted stone. He sat down on a wall and all the lousiness he felt began to overwhelm him. One of those times. Deep blues. No jobs, friends or prospects. Body abused and beginning to overheat. Self-pity awash with seediness. And inside, like a balled claw gripping his guts, there was the broken balustrade and the black horizon below. This was the place he'd seen, the place of death, and he was horrified. Jerry could not look down there again; he didn't dare consider his own demise. But from the insular broodings that the fucked-up Jerry indulged in, a kind of suicide did arise. Jerry wasn't going to be Jerry any more. With ingenuity born of necessity, like a ghost stepping from a corpse, a new person eventually stood up from the seated figure and walked off towards the rutted plain. Discernibly, this person was no different. He had the same hangdog looks and shambling gait. But there was light glimmering somewhere in the vacant eyes. Two faint lights of purpose projected towards a dim horizon. One light for a name yet to be found. Another, bitter and vengeful, for a half-realized love wrenched away.

16

There were no tamarisk trees near the base of Cofton Tower and not the slightest trace of a beach. A few litter-swamped shrubs and the rain-washed lines of builder's sand were all it had to offer. But Des was not too disheartened. The job was going well, he had news enough to satisfy a hungry Bertha. He walked briskly through the sunshine and up to the main entrance. The stinking lifts were given short shrift. Des was up the stairs in no time and knocking on Bertha's door.

'Well, mister, I reckon I've missed you.'

Before Des had time to cross the threshold, Bertha had her arms around him and was rubbing up close. It was awkward. All that intimacy out in the cold, impersonal hall. And Des knowing he wanted the impersonal but was being pulled in deep.

'Easy now, Bertha, I've only just got here.'

'You mean you're not glad to see me?'

'No, but, you know . . .'

Des reciprocated without much feeling, or rather he did so disregarding the lust that was beginning to stir. With fondling hands, he guided Bertha into pink frilliness and got her down on the sofa.

'So how come you're so hot to see me?'

'Come on, several hungry nights have passed.'

'I'm surprised you're not pissed off.'

Des plonked a few kisses on Bertha's cheeks and wished he hadn't. He wiped the make-up off and tried to work out what was going on in her eyes.

'I've learned you need a long lead, and that's all right, as long as you come back and give me my due,' she told him.

'That's what I'm here for.'

Before Bertha had a chance to pull him back down into a clinch, Des eased the photos out from beneath his shirt. This was his strategy. Divert attention and get back to strictly business.

'You might want to prepare yourself for these.'

'What are they?'

'Your daughter at work, I'd guess you'd say.'

'Oh God . . .'

The photos had their effect. Bertha sat on the sofa all straightened out with her skirt down to her knees. She didn't touch or look at Des but silently stared with damp eyes at the ridiculousness of sex. Des began to feel sorry for her yet again. This was no memory a mother needed. This was wildlife safari, copulation and death on the rutted plain.

'When you see it like this . . .'

'Yeh, nothing special in one way, but in this context, awful. I'm sorry.'

The lousiness that Des suddenly felt spread quickly. He began to think about the last time he handed over photos and posh Rebecca's quivering chin. Images worse than words, worse than witnessing infidelity. These were mere fragments of truth, compressed, ambivalent and haunting. And Des could've been the one to snap Claudette, a seedy little snooper out to break people's hearts. Fuck it, that Irish git Liam was right; we should photograph the night.

'I guess I've seen worse in my life,' Bertha lamely muttered. 'So, go on, tell me, who's the man?'

'Sir Martin Wainwright.'

'Jesus! I thought I knew the face.'

'Couldn't get anyone much bigger in the city.'

'So Claudette and maybe this Gary Marlow thought they'd make a bundle.'

'Could be, though someone else could be involved. Maybe someone else set up the session and found out what was going on.'

'And do we know who this might be?'

'Not yet. The boyfriend of the dead photographer reckons it might be a guy with part of a finger missing. That ring a bell?'

'N-No . . .'

'Then of course there's your ex, Ross Constanza. He beat the shit out of Vin St James just because Vin had the nerve to be suspicious.'

'Huh, that's Ross for you.'

'So, what do you think then, Bertha?'

She seemed to be struggling. Fingers writhing around the hem of her dress, eyes burning the carpet. When she spoke, she sounded too cool.

'I think you're doing well, Des. We now know why, and you're going to find out who, right?'

'I'm on my way.'

Des didn't get very far. It was Bertha's eyes that did it. All that pain and defiance that wouldn't turn away, that wouldn't blink or deferentially look down. She wasn't going to let him off the hook. Des felt quite detached at that moment. He knew he shouldn't, and mostly didn't want to. The job could soon be complete; he wanted a cheque and an uncluttered goodbye. He could also see that Bertha was no slave to her emotions. Temporary needs, her own sensual power and the cash made Des more than just a hired hand. He didn't know why, but Bertha had to have him doubly tied. But then his thoughts turned full circle. Shit, she was having a bad time and Des didn't feel much better. Comfort had to be grabbed wherever it came in the cold city where the only horizons are those in strangers' eyes. And so seedy photos fell to the floor and new calls of hunger were heeded. Clothes ripped off in haste. Worn flesh grappled with.

*　　*　　*

The weather had changed. The wind was up and large white clouds were bundling across the sky. Bertha watched their distorted movement in the mirrored glass of the Hyatt as she sat in City Square waiting for Paddy Conroy. It seemed to her a strange place to meet, but Paddy had been adamantly against going to a pub. Still trying to keep off the sauce, or maybe it was just too intimate, thought Bertha. Paddy did have an experiential edge over Des McGinlay. She looked around the empty brick spaces and struggled to light up a fag. The buffeting wind and the comforting cigarette seemed to sum up her mood. Comfort that she still had Des on board and proof near at hand. But a disturbing swirl of feeling too, as she thought once more of the photo and Ross Constanza's four-fingered hand, which was surely somewhere behind it. It didn't seem a question of old anger but one of profound grievance in the here and now. But Bertha tried to keep those feelings back. She knew she needed a plan and a cool mind to carry it out. Paddy Conroy planted his sturdy backside down next to her.

'You've got a bloom to your cheeks there, Bertha.'

'It feels more like frostbite, you arsehole.'

'Just being courteous.'

'Sounds like that woman has got you tied up in knots.'

'It's for my own good. I had a stroke a while back.'

Paddy was wearing a crumpled cream suit and a bright blue shirt that was stretched tight against his gut. He sought to smooth the thin strands of hair he had left but eventually gave up. Bertha didn't think he was a patch on Des.

'So what are these developments you spoke of, Bertha?'

'It goes something like this, Paddy. Ross has built up this business of providing tarts to high-class punters. Now, one of these high-class punters got set up and was put in a very compromising position. Well, you know Ross and his extreme solutions. He's been trying to murder his way out of trouble and it hasn't come off.'

'How come you know about this?'

'I've got a guy working for me. We've got the compromising information and near enough proof against Ross.'

'Is this to do with Claudette's death?'

'You knew?'

'Didn't like to say anything when you came round that time but . . . I'm really sorry, Bertha.'

'Ross was in at the birth and in at the death.'

'I guess you've got cause enough to want him fixed.'

Bertha looked at the distorted clouds and the windswept square. She shivered with disquiet.

'It seems like it's everything, Paddy. What he did to me then, what he's done to me now and what he's deprived me of in between.'

'So what have you got in mind?'

Bertha paused briefly. 'Well, it wouldn't do just to bump him off, or get him nicked.'

'Hah, that's no easy task, Bertha.'

'I've got someone in mind who might do it, this guy who works for me, but I was thinking first that we should try and take the business off him.'

'You mean kind of blackmail him out of it?'

'Why not? If we've got him linked to murder . . .'

'It won't be easy.'

'. . . And I've got some cash. With your help we could set ourselves up with a nice number.'

'I don't know. It's nice in theory, but in practice – well think of the man, Bertha. You know him well enough.'

Bertha felt a stab of anger. Paddy had gone all soft, tucked away in the suburbs and wanting the quiet life, no doubt holding on till some friggin pension becomes due.

'Come on, Paddy, you want the guy, there's money in it too. Those cheap sauna joints you run can't pay that much.'

'So what do I have to do?'

'Nothing. I'll do the doing but I need you as a backer.'

'I guess, in a way, I owe you one.'

'Let's shake on a renewed friendship.'

Paddy Conroy had cold damp hands. That hadn't used to be true. The way it goes downhill. Bertha felt another stab of anger.

'Fuck it, Paddy, we're stuck and we need change!'

* * *

It was nice not to be stuffing a raucous balti down your throat, feeling the ghee clog your ventricles and wadding in naan against the chilli burn. This was civilized. A tablecloth, napkins and a cute little basket of garlic bread. Des didn't know where to put his hands, though he secretly knew where he wanted to. Pearl sat opposite him looking glorious in the intimate peach light that shone from the walls. She wore a tight-fitting black dress with an amber brooch which matched her hair perfectly. Des looked into Chinese eyes and thought of clippers sailing the seas of Trinidad, ships from all over the world made one in those eyes. Soft bastard, he thought.

'You want to tell me about your week?' Pearl said.

'Private investigator?'

'Yeh.'

'Not really. It's shit-shovelling, dirty deeds and dirty thoughts and not a lot to feel proud about.'

143

'You make money.'

'Yeh, s'pose so, and it beats driving a taxi or working in a bar, but . . . well, I guess the dirt's wearing off on me.'

'I know the feeling.'

'You want to talk about your work?'

'Nah, it's the same story. Shitty, fucked up people, a shitty pimp who screws with my mind.'

'My, what a pair we are!'

It was an Italian restaurant, and Des went with a pasta and chicken concoction. He made an effort to eat in a composed way. So did Pearl and the result was laughter.

'Are you trying to make out I'm really a pig?'

'It's obvious, Des. Go on, be yourself. Shovel it in.'

'Of course, you went to some finishing school down south.'

'I know all about etiquette.'

'Etiquette. What a bloody stupid word.'

'I like it, Des. It reminds me of manicured fingers lifting titchy china cups, rich blue-rinse ladies talking posh, you know, afternoon piano sessions and never having to clean the loo.'

'Such people don't need to go to the loo, they're so refined.'

'Don't you think it would be nice to be so above it all?'

'With you . . . yeh.'

Pearl gave off a sweet smile that made Des quiver down to his shoes. It was a good sensation. What the future might hold ceased to concern him.

'Let's imagine we've all the time in the world.'

'You're reading my thoughts, Pearl.'

'That's a good sign.'

'Like just sitting here and enjoying ourselves.'

'No dirty thoughts.'

'Well, a few maybe, but nicely restrained.'

'You sweet me and I'll sweet you.'

'Sounds fine to me . . .'

And so it went on, a languid night in a restaurant until they were kicked out at closing time. A strange feeling that Des had with Pearl of wanting but not wanting to touch her. Warm smiles in the dark as he drove her home, smiles not seen but felt. He stopped outside her house. In the streetlight, Des saw Pearl raise a thin eyebrow and smile. 'All the time in the world, eh?' he said, their hands briefly touching and then Pearl slipping away from him. Des didn't drive off straight away. He bathed a little in the good vibes he felt, looked up at the streetlight glow and almost believed it was the sun.

17

You don't phone a bigwig like Sir Martin Wainwright and expect a meeting. The only thing to do is doorstep. So, not so bright but early, Des headed out of the city to the leafy lanes where most bigwigs live, leafy lanes with no names and long sweeping drives equally anonymous. It was a disconcerting experience. No pavements, or people. Wide tilting spaces being sucked off into a cavernous sky. Dense greenery flopping down over dark places where some kind of pain lurked. Des hunched over the steering wheel and kept his eyes close to the road. It took quite a long time before he found the right discreet drive with its locked iron gates. He stared at a phone and video camera. The signs of privilege and unequal exchange. The ultimate put-down. Des wouldn't have used the system, even if he thought he could get in. A field full of cows beckoned.

Thoughts of Pearl kept him going. Smooth amber brightly glowing in a cosy place where memories had been banned. That restrained anticipation of delight got him through the squalor of the field. The midges and thistles, the shit and blowflies, the mad-eyed cows gushing piss. He made it to the security of a copse of trees and a wooden fence topped with barbed wire. But this didn't prove much of a barrier. An overhanging branch provided a lift up and Des soon worked his way over. Then he was crunching forecourt gravel, feeling more at home, and running his fingers along the lines of a Jaguar. He reached for the front door bell. Des kicked the mud off his shoes and smiled.

The housekeeper who answered the door was not pleased. 'How did you get here?' she said belligerently. The backwoods twang seemed comical to Des.

'Walked up the drive.' Des smiled. 'Your gates are wide open.'

'What? Well, they shouldn't be, and you shouldn't be here.'

'You'd better send someone down to sort it out then, and in the meantime, you can announce me to Sir Martin.'

'What? Well, who are you?'

'McGinlay, private investigator.' Des pulled out a grubby card. 'I'm engaged in a private and delicate matter that Sir Martin alone knows about, so, you'd better inform him I'm here. It concerns a certain Claudette Turton.'

Des was beginning to enjoy himself. Talking to a maid no less! He stuffed his hands in his trouser pockets and grinned. She looked apprehensive but eventually scuttled off, leaving Des to gaze at a rusty suit of armour that seemed to serve as a hat stand. After a few minutes, a pale beanpole of a man in a black suit came into the hall, evidently to keep an eye out. But Des wasn't perturbed. He cast his eyes around the candy-striped hall and thought Sir Martin's pile was no huge deal. Six bedrooms maybe, who gives a fuck? And then the maid returned, her brow a spider's web of frowns.

'Sir Martin will see you. Will you please come this way, sir?' she said with half-hearted politeness.

Des smiled anyway and ambled his way after her.

'I admire your etiquette,' he said as he was shown into a side room.

Sir Martin was, well, grey. He had a full crop of grey hair, a neatly clipped grey moustache and he wore a grey suit. His face, too, was tinged with grey. He didn't look any

147

different from the pictures in the newspapers – as if the guy was walking front-page news. He sat at a small table and beckoned Des to sit down.

'I don't really know why I'm doing this, Mr – er – McGinlay. I don't recall ever having requested your services. However, I do sometimes have reason to turn to private investigators so maybe your name has slipped my mind.'

Sir Martin was getting flabby. But Des didn't need the tight suit to tell him that. He'd seen photos of the real thing. He put his hand inside his coat and felt the envelope. Sir Martin's burnt-umber eyes waited, burnt eyes above a high-boned precipice of pitted flesh, a mouth resolutely small. Des hesitated. He didn't feel comfortable with the eyes, feeling there was something odd about them, distant but also rudely penetrating. Des felt himself shrinking back but he managed to check himself. Sod the deference, he thought, and so launched in.

'It's a difficult situation this.' Des fumbled for a fag and then lit up. The room was practically empty, a kind of cold-shoulder reception place for tradesmen and the unwanted such as himself.

'I've been on this case, chasing a bare arse halfway across the city and not knowing who it belonged to. But it seemed like an important arse because two people who saw it ended up dead.'

The grey face remained impassive and the eyes still drilled, though Des thought he saw a slight smile beneath the clipped moustache.

'Now of course, I don't believe that this arse has the capacity to shoot bullets or anything like that. I mean, I guess you could say that it's just a good-time arse having fun.'

'I think you'd better get to the point, Mr McGinlay.'

'You're right.' Des slipped the envelope across the table. 'Take a look inside. I'm sure you've seen them before. Did

148

Claudette mail them through the post to you, or did she nobble you outside your political headquarters?'

Sir Martin was a man of perfected calm, Teflon exterior. His trade no doubt cultivated that. He looked at the photos and then dismissively pushed them away.

'Fakes, Mr McGinlay. I'm sorry you've wasted your time.' The mouth hardly moved beneath the moustache.

'Come on . . .' Des was nearly speechless. 'Is that what you're going to say to the police and press when I hand these bleedin prints in?'

'Such fabrications have been known. It's easy to transpose one face for another, happens all the time in the photographic world.'

'Bullshit.'

Silence descended on the room. The almost motionless Sir Martin stared down at the table; only his little finger moved, waggling the air like a flailing worm. Des let him work out an angle. He looked out of a small window and got a view of a swimming pool.

'Maybe, and without conceding anything, maybe I should buy these photos from you, these and any others there might be. A worthwhile sum that reflects their collector's value?'

'Yeh, that's interesting. And what is the going rate for collectable porn?'

'Shall we say . . . two thousand?'

'Mmmm, that's not bad for a few prints.'

'Well, you look like a man who could do with a few extra bob. It's a grubby business at the sharp end, making ends meet. I've been there myself a long time ago.'

'Well, I guess it's an option I should keep under review . . .'

And Des did see the possibilities. A bit of bargaining and he could make it five. Almost half a year's pay and a chance to bugger off to a sun-soaked island. Pearl on the beach drinking spiced wine. But that thought became alarming. Pearl was a dream. The job, he knew, was his only reality.

'. . . But keep under review only along with all the other aspects of this case.'

'I'm sure there is nothing else I can contribute.'

'Well, it would be nice to know how you met Claudette. I presume someone set it up for you. The nice Mr Constanza maybe, or was it Gary Marlow? And it would be nice to know who did the blackmailing and who said they'd sort it out for you?'

'There's nothing more I can say.'

'Maybe I'm getting a bit too complicated. Maybe it was just you, Mr Wainwright, who bumped off Claudette and Mary Holmes?'

The big businessman and Euro bête noire stood abruptly. His umber eyes spat contempt as he went over to the door and pressed a buzzer. Then he turned, his face more ashen but his eyes exuding cold power.

'This is the last time we meet, Mr McGinlay. Any further interaction you might wish, deal with my lawyer. Just take your filthy dross and bugger off!'

Des rose too and stashed the photos away. He realized then that it would be sensible if he got copies made.

'It's up to you, Mr Wainwright. Help me and I'll see if I can keep it all quiet. Go with your procurer and the whole world will know what a dirty fucker you are. A dirty fucker who'd kill to keep his reputation clean.'

Des walked out of the room, just as several men came down the hall to usher him out.

'I'll give you a day to come up with a reply,' he called back defiantly.

And so Des left the sanctuary of wealth and went back to the city. A sliver of fear pierced him as he drove and it made his heart flutter. He realized his knees were shaking. *Jesus. Who knows what a guy like that could do?* Then he looked out and saw gentle hills in the distance, viridian-washed beneath charcoal skies. It seemed a lifetime since he'd seen such things. They didn't mean anything.

* * *

The Jag and the Bentley were parked carelessly on the grass space at the end of an unmetalled lane. Two men stood by the cars, their hands thrust in pockets, their shoulders hunched against an unseasonable chill wind. The lane ended abruptly at a ten-foot chain-link fence. Behind this there was a long, squat line of lights that marked the end of the airport runway. In the distance, the terminus could be seen and behind its white tower, the whole enormous spread of the city.

'Bit fucking dramatic, ennit, coming up here? Jesus, these sort of places give me the creeps.'

'Well, Ross, the situation demands extreme caution.'

'Huh, any bleeding snooper with binoculars could watch us. It took me ages to find the place.'

'I used to own a section of this land and made a million plus selling it.'

'Most people reminisce about their sexual conquests.'

'Yes, well maybe I should've stuck to land deals. We have a deeply serious situation on hand.'

Sir Martin Wainwright leaned back onto the bonnet of his Jaguar and looked over at a jet airliner being hauled to a far-off terminus. He clenched his teeth and then told Ross Constanza about a certain private eye.

'Oh no . . .' Ross groaned and ground his foot into the turf. He wished he hadn't. The turf was squelchy. It seemed indicative of the sinking feeling in his gut. He looked sideways at Wainwright. Dark-eyed and cold; dangerously so, and not to be underestimated. 'I did hear of someone snuffling around, but he didn't seem to be getting anywhere.'

151

'You should've told me. He's knocking on my door, Ross.'

'I thought we'd covered all the angles, but some of the snaps must've got into third-party hands that none of us knew about.'

'All of this is your fault.'

'Come on . . . I'll sort it. It's a loose end that can be quickly snipped.'

'I want no more killing. You didn't tell me about the photographer.'

'It was a mistake. She just flipped and had an accident.'

'I want this McGinlay deprived of the photos or forced to do a deal. Nothing more.'

'I'll handle it myself.'

'You'll do it properly or else all the deals we might have in the pipeline are off.'

'That's my motivation, Wainwright. Otherwise, who gives a shit if you hit the *News of the World*?'

'Don't –' Sir Martin suddenly pressed a pointing finger at Ross. 'Don't get cheap with me, Constanza. I've got you well and truly trussed should any of this get out.'

'Look, you made the deal with Claudette in the first place. If you'd've come through me there would've been security. Jesus, it's me who's helping you out of a hole.'

'OK, she was highly persuasive and I was reckless, but don't forget we're both tied together.'

A plane began to descend onto a runway on the far side of the airport. Sir Martin watched it for a few moments, unfazed by the open space, and then looked at his watch. 'I've got to go. Day full of meetings, I'm afraid.' He opened the door of his Jaguar. 'I want a regular update on developments, OK?'

Ross watched the car drive off, then turned and looked at the airfield. What a wind shit of a place, he thought with a shudder, and a shit situation, as shitty as when I landed in the nick. He knew then he should've ditched Wainwright the moment he was told of Claudette's scam. God, he should've joined in with her and bled the bugger dry. Ross felt his shoulders sag. He could well have backed the wrong side, but knew he had no choice but to see things through. He looked down at his soggy shoes and then over at the airport terminal. Too much open space. Vulnerable to sniper fire. Makes your head spin.

*   *   *

She had short shaven orange hair, a nose full of rings and a large stomach that squeezed out of a tatty black T-shirt. Her breasts were quite large too, flopping at all angles as she got ready to lift. But Jerry was most taken with her eyes, pale blue and playful, inquisitive but non-judgemental. He grabbed his end of the mattress and was already beginning to feel at home.

'OK, you just keep it up and I'll pull.'

And another thing, this woman was strong. She braced her silver Docs onto the stairs and easily heaved the mattress up, almost pulling Jerry with her.

'One more pull and we'll be on the first landing.'

Since first arriving with his stuff, she'd taken more things up the two flights of stairs than Jerry, carrying two boxes of books to his one. This was perhaps just as well since Jerry felt frail and run-down, and a simple walk up the stairs made him puff.

'W-We g-going to be able to get this round the c-corner?'

'A piece of piss. When I get it on the landing, we'll pull it round fast so it doesn't stick.'

'Sounds l-like you've d-done it before.'

'In this place, loads of times. We get more turnover than the YHA.'

She braced herself again ready to pull.

It was a stroke of luck that Jerry should be doing what he

was. Out on Argent Street, wandering like a lost dog, he'd met a casual acquaintance and blurted out he was fearful of going home. 'I c-can still see her, m-man, all m-mashed up,' he kept saying. The guy he'd met, Paul, happened to be one of those people whose connections spread wide around the city. He knew all about 65 Anselm Road.

'It's a long-established squat, man. Been going years. Owned by some rich old dear who can't get her act together. You'll get a room there, man. The people are cool, yeh. They'll help you get through the shit.'

Jerry wasn't sure he wanted that kind of help, but he knew he had to move away to stop himself totally flipping. Then it was a question of following Paul around a few pubs until he was introduced to Jed, one of the long-term squatters, who readily offered him a room. Jerry then persuaded Frederick to drive his stuff over, a pile of cases and boxes crammed in the old Ford with the mattress flopping around on the roof rack. It all happened so fast and yet it felt to Jerry as if it was part of a plan. He gave a huge sigh of relief when Frederick drove away. A strange house in an unfamiliar part of the city. It was all right.

'OK, this is the last pu-lll!'

From the top of the second set of stairs, the woman practically ran the mattress into Jerry's new room, and pulled him along too. Then she let go and let it slap against the dusty carpet. She followed, bouncing down on her back, her breasts spreading like liquid jelly and her belly wobbling like the set kind.

'Wow, I think I've earned a rest.'

'Y-You've b-been great. Thanks a lot.'

She hitched herself up onto an elbow and Jerry once more warmed to her eyes.

'So what are you in here for?' she asked.

'Er, I d-dunno, ch-chuck out the old and s-starting anew.'

'Any particular reason?'

154

Jerry nodded but couldn't speak.

'S'all right, tell me some other time. I tell you, we've all got problems here.'

'Y-Yeah?'

'Jed's on methadone, trying to kick the habit but not doing that great. He can't get a job and keeps getting ill all the time. As for me, I'm on the run. Running from a lousy childhood in the dark and boring suburbs. And, well, knocking down any sacred cow I come across and there's a bleedin mountain of them about.'

Jerry began to look around the room, knowing he couldn't think of much more to say. The woman sensed this and stood up. She bounced in her Docs on the mattress.

'The name's Mouse by the way,' she said.

'M-Mouse?'

'We all take weird names here. What's yours?'

'Er, dunno. F-Fred?'

'Ha, you don't sound too sure.'

'Any old n-name I reckon.'

'Yeh, well I'm going to call you – Stray. That seems to me what you are.'

'Yeh, why not?'

Mouse bounced off the mattress and clumped over to the door. 'I'll check you later, OK? Stray?'

'F-Fine.'

The room was reasonable enough. Not too small and with a nice sloping roof. It even had clean wallpaper, although the marks left by picture frames and furniture were a bit disconcerting. His window was at the front of the house and he had a clear view of the road. The only problem was the large tree on the opposite side. Jerry felt sure pigeons would be lodged there. Their irritating noise seemed to be all around. But it was reasonable enough; it was an escape and a chance to start again. He sat down on the mattress amid his possessions. A new life, a new name even, and a chance to re-enter the world in a different way. Jerry smiled brightly.

'A m-missing fucking p-person, what c-can you m-make out of that?'

And then a fierce spurt of bile rushed through him as he caught a glimpse once more of the battered Mary and the horny face of that politician.

'Sh-Shit . . .'

Jerry stood up shaking. He began to wander around the room. And then he stopped and stared at a pale square where someone else's picture used to be. He started to cry.

18

'So, how's it going, Wayne?'

'Same as ever, mate. Three stiffs from down the morgue most nights and the brewery's getting restless.'

'The last of the last legs, eh?'

'You said it.'

'So where's Dick then? He makes up the numbers.'

'Ha-ha, there's a bleedin story. The bloke's been nicked.'

'What?'

'Too right, got done for flashin. Can you believe it? Indecent exposure, bloody crazy.'

'Jesus, Wayne.'

'I mean, it just goes to show, you can know a bloke for years, on the other side of the bar, but it don't mean you know him at all, you get me?'

'Yeh. Guess you could say that about a lot of situations. So where'd he get caught waving his willy then?'

'Fuck knows.'

Des picked up the two whiskies from the bar. He smiled to himself as he imagined Dick O'Malley doing his thing. Desperate times.

'By the way, any calls for me, Wayne?'

'Some guy called asking about you. Didn't want to leave his name, though.'

Des sat down in the far corner of the bar and slid a glass of whisky over to Errol. He looked up at the walls since he knew that Errol was fuming. Time to let things cool down. Des perused Louis Armstrong's clowning face and then the smoke-filled eyes of Lester Young. *Personality, doesn't it warm the cockles of your heart to have all these familiar faces with you always?* He eased down in his seat and began to inspect the whisky's golden glow.

'Look, Des, don't try an fuckin ignore it. You've pissed me about, man.'

'Don't see why.'

'You've got vital evidence, for fuck's sake!'

'You'll get the photos, Errol. It's only a matter of timing.'

'We were gonna get together and work this through. So what happen? You collar this Jerry git before we do, then he goes and disappears. You get important evidence off him, then won't give it in or show it. That is sheer fuck'ry, man!'

'I told you, I'm just getting some copies made.'

'What is it with you? You don't trust me?'

Des lit himself a fag. He noticed Errol's hair was beginning to thin and his cheeks were sinking inwards. *The trouble with knowing someone a long time, you see yourself getting old.*

'Well just tell me something, Errol, right? Up there in the hierarchy of our magnificent police, what will they do about the photos of Sir Martin Wainwright having a kinky screw?'

'Probably nothing.'

'Right!'

'It's not illegal, Des, having a fuck, and the photos could be seen as an invasion of privacy.'

'Jesus! Ain't it always for the sirs of this world?'

'I'm just sayin, man –'

'Come on, Errol, these photos make Wainwright a murder suspect!'

'All the more reason you hand them in!'

158

'Yeh, and have them sat on by some fraternal mason's arse!'

An edgy silence returned. Errol frowned hard at the table and sucked his teeth. Des would've liked to have taken a photo then. Worry. Vexation. That should be the sort of thing shoved on walls. Everyday lunacies, self-portraits of ordinary lives. Des eased forward and held out his hands in entreaty.

'Come on, let's start again, huh? This whole thing's getting off-limits for the police, and that's the place I can function.'

'Dangerous and mad, Des.'

'No, you can hold the rope for me, right, mate? I'll give you the photos and any other evidence I can get too and together we can pull it all in and nab the bastards.'

'And who are the bastards?'

'Dunno yet.'

'Great.'

'Face it, Errol, I'm more likely to find out than you, I mean, with this bigwig involved.'

'True.'

'I just need a few more connections and then we'll know how to play it.'

'Well, it all sounds like a load of bollocks.'

It was Errol's turn to ease back then. He pushed against the fake leather seat, gave his tie a tweak and wearily smiled at Des.

'So why ya doin dis, man?' he said in his Jamaican voice. 'You gonna get you'self kill.'

'Dunno, Errol. You get into it and you can't stop.' Des looked up at Louis Armstrong. 'I mean, if I did stop, what would I be looking at? A big pile of nothing, Errol, and spiders crawling down the wall.'

*   *   *

He was definitely losing them, no doubt about it. Ross felt he could almost hear the marbles rolling down the windpipe and clunking like gallstones in Scobie's gut. He's had that stupid grin on his face for days. The guy has got to go. Ross sighed. Look at the fucker now, one eye on his curly fringe, the other trying to give Mount Everest the come-on.

'How did I end up with so much shit?'

'What d'you say, boss?'

'Never mind.'

Ross Constanza was feeling as miserable as he'd ever felt in years. From the moment his eyes had first seen light that morning, a big cloud had followed him round. He couldn't get it up with his girlfriend. He couldn't eat any breakfast. His office had seemed like a poxy cell full of niggles and bad vibes. For the first time in ages he felt like shoving it all. 'Hard man Ross' was a bloody great laugh.

'I've got a bad feeling about this Wainwright business, Scobie. I don't like it at all.'

'Reckon you should let the bugger sink. I would.'

'We're in too deep. If he gets fucked, so do we.'

'So what you want me to do then?'

'There's this dick, McGinlay, he's got some of those snaps of our famous friend.'

'And we want em back pronto?'

'Right. But get this, Scobie, we want them back without any more blood spilled, right? You can teeth them, or do a deal with the git, but we can't afford any more dead bodies. Has that penetrated your friggin thick skull?'

'Sure, I ain't gotta do the guy in.'

'I've been doing a bit of checking. He hangs around the Fedora a bit, got a pad off Argent Street and is buddies with a well-up tec in the police.'

'Who's paying the fuck?'

'Not sure yet, but I can make a good guess.'

160

'OK, boss, I'm on it.'

'You got it clear what I want now, Scobie?'

'Yeh, yeh, no dead bodies.'

Scobie got off his chair, gave his hair a flick as he passed a mirror by the door and then went out of the office. Ross hugged himself. First chance, he thought, feed that git to the wolves.

Gus then poked his head into the office. 'You got a visitor, boss.'

Ross looked up. The big black cloud had walked right through the doorway.

'Why did I think I might see you again?'

'Guilty conscience probably.'

'And what's that?'

'Ha, see you haven't changed.'

'Well, it must be nigh on twenty years since we last mixed it and you certainly have changed. But that's the curse of a lot of women, though, ain't it? Big bums and big tums. Sagging tits and double chins.'

'Still as charming as ever, I see.'

It had been in the back of his mind, somewhere, that Bertha Turton would turn up on his doorstep. There could be no direct connection. He felt sure she couldn't have known. But like Vin St James, Ross had thought that Bertha would come prying about the loss of the daughter whore. One more headache in what was becoming a migraine world.

'So, Bertha, what is it I can do for you? Need a new outlet for your secretarial skills?'

'You're not that far off actually, Ross. I am looking for a new outlet but word-processing wasn't what I had in mind.'

Ross kept his mouth shut. There was a determined edge to Bertha's voice which he didn't like. He noticed, too, that she was wearing what seemed like expensive clothes. A cream and brown kit with padded shoulders and a gold necklace that looked full carat. Maybe she wasn't just a mousy nobody in a council flat any more. Ross decided to feign compassion.

'I was very sorry to hear about Claudette, you know.'

'I'm sure you were, Ross.'

'Really, when it happened, I thought about you, us, the fun we had before the shit hit the fan.'

'Jesus, Ross, the way you –' Bertha suddenly stopped herself. She took a cigarette out of her bag and lit up. She gave Ross a hard stare.

'Sod this conversation. I never pushed it, the question of who the guy was, but it could well have been that out of the fun we had, Ross, out of the fun came Claudette.'

'Now wait –'

'You wait. The point has to be made that Claudette may have been your daughter. The fact that has to be faced is that you may have killed your own flesh and blood!'

'Jesus, fuck. You stupid bitch, who d'you think you are, coming in pointing the bleeding finger? I haven't killed anyone!'

'I'm onto you, Ross. I know what it's all about and I reckon you owe me, twice over now, and you're going to pay!'

'This is a ridiculous conversation.' Ross stood up abruptly. He felt his whole body clench as he walked a few steps to stand looking out of his small office window.

'I'm not going to let go of this,' Bertha said to his back.

Ross ignored the comment. He had a view of tarmac and the grilled roller doors of an empty industrial unit. It seemed a strangely comforting view compared to what was behind him. A black cloud in a confined space and the walls moving in. An ex-lover still resentful and out to get him. He smiled to himself. The way to conduct a

162

conversation with the past. The way to face up to its unwanted and ugly return. He let his eyes focus on the horizontal lines of the warehouse doors as if he was watching a malfunctioning TV.

'Bertha,' he said wearily, 'I don't care what you think or suspect me of, and I certainly don't care about things that happened way back. So let's cut that shit out. You've come here – you haven't changed I'm sure – you've come here with some angle so you might as well spit the bleeder out and then we can talk.'

'Yeh, it's probably best to keep it impersonal. Strictly business, as you used to say when you screwed around. I want back in, Ross. I want my cut of what I had before. The escort business – girls, punters, files, the lot. I've got money and a backer, and you know, full well you know, I could run things far better than you.'

Ross sighed loudly. Bomb the bleedin lot, he thought. Exterminate and scarper . . . but where the bloody hell to?

'Very interesting, Bertha, funny even,' he said aloud. 'So tell me, why should I give this crap more than a few seconds thought?'

'Huh, I used to stroke your balls, Ross. Now I can cut them off.'

* * *

It was his first venture out of the squat as Fred Stray. All very alarming. The two spliffs he'd smoked seemed to have given him no protection. Jerry felt like a child out on the streets alone for the first time. He stood in the dark shadows of the old house and tried to work out which way to go. This was strange territory. A zone of the city where he was already lost. The solid trees presented the first problem. Trunks large enough to hide a man. Foliage dense, matted and eerily fissured with streaks of light. Jerry tentatively moved forward towards the pavement. The windows of the houses became apparent. The eyes of the street. Some brazenly shining, others pitch black and threatening. He almost retreated but a comforting thought eased its way into his fretful mind. Some kind of past remembrance of when the snow was thick and pavements had to be abandoned. A time when, as a child, he'd followed the thin lines of tyres right up the middle of the road. It seemed to present a solution. Jerry lowered his head, stepped between parked cars and imagined he could see tracks leading off into the night.

Mouse had given him the idea. They seemed to have hit it off straight away and she'd visited his room for a number of chats.

'You can't just sit and mope,' she said. 'Brooding is a kind of living death. This bleedin room could end up a coffin. You've got to get it out of you, Stray, be in the world in whatever way you can.'

Jerry got the stutters bad then. He could hardly get any words together other than, 'What the f-f-fuck w-was out th-there in the f-f-first p-place!'

A spark of anger glinted in Mouse's eyes and she kicked out in Jerry's direction with a heavy boot.

'Don't be such a defeatist runt! What is there? Well, for one thing there's the shitbags who killed your woman. Are you going to let them just fester? You may not be able to do much, but you could do something, even if it's just kicking in a few car lights.'

Mouse was all for action, hyper-action almost, and she didn't seem to give anything a second thought. This, Jerry could just about see, was the kind of influence he needed, though the thought of him doing something seemed remote. Dope and depression just meant more dreams and anxieties laid out face up on a carpeted floor. But Jerry fought the urge to wallow. He did see the possibilities offered by a violent act, the frustrations it could purge. So, that evening, with the darkness down and the streets empty, Jerry got off his arse and went out for a dry run.

It all went smoothly at first. There were no cars or people about. Walking down the middle of the road, he felt a sense of freedom and a kind of immunity. This enabled him to think, to think positively and not to brood. He vowed to seek revenge, any act of revenge, big or small, against those who had killed Mary. He didn't know what he could do or how. He thought that maybe Mouse would help, and that out of it would come a new direction to his life.

This unexpected glimpse of optimism made him smile, but it was short-lived. The bright glare of headlights and a loud horn shocked him back to reality. He had to jump for the pavement as a car accelerated past. Someone inside the car shouted, 'Yer stupid fucker!' Jerry felt disorientated. The front door to a house opened and he saw a burly silhouette looking out at him. He began to rush along the pavement. He became conscious of the trees and of the strange dripping noises they made. Then he ran and came to a stretch of parkland. The blackness was inviting. Jerry crept in.

He stalled. An animal, a dog maybe or a fox, was standing on the grass in front of him. Two eyes, glinting with streetlight, yellow and malevolent, were staring right at him. And then it came. The snow, grey snow this time, filtering through the darkness like ash from the death-throes of a fire. Jerry collapsed.

19

'This is a shitty job, you know that, Des. Goes completely against my principles.'

'I surely know it, Liam.'

'I mean, this is smut, tacky smut and it's not very well done either.'

'Well, the fifty quid should at least ease the pain.'

'You're corrupting me, man.'

Liam was arranging a set of lights over a table in the resource centre's photography room. One of Liam's offspring was also there, fiddling around with drying spools and bits of old film. Des kept a cautious eye out, prepared to believe the kid would wreck the place.

'The thing I've got to do is not get any reflection or shadow. Difficult when you haven't got all the right gear.'

'Don't worry too much, as long as you get the basics.'

'You mean the faces and the fucking.'

'Perfectly put.'

There was a sudden crashing noise behind them. Des raised his eyes to the ceiling. Liam didn't even look up.

'Stop pissing about, you stupid bugger!' he shouted.

'But I'm bored, Dad!'

'I told you to do a bit of drawing on the table over there.'

'Bloody hell! Them're dirty pictures!' The kid had poked his head around Des and was ogling at Sir Martin's happy hour.

'Get back to that table and mind your own business!'

Des eased the boy out of the way and gave off one of his hard-man stares. It did the trick. He turned back to Liam, wondering whether he'd chosen the right person for the job. 'This gonna be much longer?'

'Ten minutes at the most.'

While Liam fretted over getting the lighting right and set up a camera stand, Des sat at a worktable, one eye on the kid, and pulled out an envelope. He addressed it to Miranda. Then he wrote out a cheque for the cost of her windscreen and began to write a note to go with it. His intention was to send off one of the snapshots too as a form of insurance in case the worst should happen. He hadn't really dared to think about the 'worst', but he was aware that this was the sort of thing you were supposed to do. Sending it to Miranda was awkward, though. She could well trash it, or come back and complain he was trying out emotional blackmail.

'*In the event of something happening to me* . . . What is this, Des? What tricks are you up to now?'

Des cringed. Maybe deep down he did see it as a way of getting back in with her?

He gave Liam's restless kid a scowl and finally wrote: 'Just keep this safe, yeh? No comebacks. Show it to Errol if you feel the need.'

Pretty lousy, but it would have to do. By then Liam had finished shooting copies of the prints. Des took one and put it in the envelope. The other he stashed in his shirt.

'So how long you reckon then, Liam?'

'I'll get the negs processed now, mate, the sprog willing, and then leave them to dry. Some time this afternoon I'll print them up for you.'

'No one's gotta know about this.'

'Fifty quid'll keep me quiet.'

'You could be in danger if someone did find out.'

'Jesus, don't put the shits up me, man. It's just an odd job on the side, right?'

'If it makes you feel better, and a fifty quid bonus if it works out OK . . .'

'Wow. Now did I put a film in the camera or not?'

Des walked back to Argent Street.

He kept his head low, following a trail of chewing gum, the odd spot of phlegm and the usual stirrings of litter. He was trying to think of his next move but felt at a loss. Constanza seemed the main candidate to check but he hadn't come up with much that made a direct connection. He wondered whether he should go back to Pauline and her psycho bodyguard of a boyfriend. She at least knew more than she'd let on. The prospect didn't enthral him and was soon forgotten. On the corner of his street, a Jaguar sat waiting, and as he approached, its rear door opened wide. Des knew what was expected. He calmly sat in the back and got a whiff of real leather. He realized that maybe he didn't need to search but that those involved would surely come to him. And there was one, the thinly clipped moustache and the seriously grey face presenting Des with another move.

'Following me, are you?'

'I was going to call, but then I saw you in the street, looking like a washed-out derelict wandering about.'

'It's what it does to me, thinking.'

'Huh-uh, and what has this thinking come up with in terms of my offer?'

'Ah, well that one's slipped away, got lost a bit.'

'You'd be a fool to turn it down. This business, it's not yours, is it? This is just a job for you with a pay day at the end of it.'

'I didn't say I'd turned it down, Sir Martin, just somehow mislaid the thought of it. But you're wrong about it being just money. The itch –' Des began to scratch at his armpit '– this bleeding itchy curiosity thing, it gets to you. You want to know answers and you know you can't stop scratching till you do. It's bad, no doubt about it; it throws money out the window.'

Des looked out of the window. The presence of a Jag in his neighbourhood was attracting some attention and he felt somehow that being in it wouldn't do his reputation any good. Sir Martin stopped leaning around in his seat and focused on the rear-view mirror instead. The burnt eyes seemed more threatening that way.

'I suppose I could tell you all you want to know. It would just be hearsay since there's no proof. Perhaps that can be the deal, McGinlay? I'll give you the money, name the names and you return the photos?'

'That is tempting, I must say.'

'So?'

'I'd have to speak to my client first.'

The brow in the rear-view mirror furrowed and the dark eyes became intense.

'I'm getting extremely annoyed with you, McGinlay. You don't seem to realize the clout I have. I can get the police to remove your licence. I can get the media to ignore those photos. I can get you killed if need be. So let's stop the prevarications, shall we? I want the photos by the end of the day or else I do all I can to finish you. That plain enough?'

Des certainly found the gaze intimidating. He was looking at power and a sense of fear began to rise in his gut. He knew also that this was just a play; it was the force of a privileged personality and the substance of the threat could well be less strong. Even so, Des struggled to give as good as he'd received. He smiled as casually as he could and opened the car door.

'Be careful now, Sir Martin. Think who's got most to lose.

You corner me, what the fuck do I care if we both go down?'

Des eased out of the car and felt the relief of cool air on his sweating face.

*   *   *

'So how c-come I never see you eat?' Jerry said as he lay back on the bed stark naked.

'Guess I don't have much of an appetite. I mean, food, you don't know where the stuff comes from, do you?'

'B-But, you know, M-Mouse, y-you are . . . w-well b-built.'

'Jesus, don't you start. I mean, all this fucking sizeism crap, it –'

'N-No, d-don't get me wrong, I l-love it. You've g-got tits like s-soft ripe squashes, a b-belly like a volup-t-t-uous b-blancmange and an arse . . . Jesus, y-you're all soft and fruitful and really d-delicious.'

'Keep saying that and I might eat you.'

'Yeh? D-Do it, Mouse.'

'Well, you certainly seem to be feeling better.'

'I guess that's d-down to you, and this.'

'What makes you flip like that, Stray? You were a complete quivering wreck.'

'I d-dunno, it's like, there's s-something st-stuck. I dunno, like inside there's a hole, a d-deep well or something and I'm c-constantly fearful I'm g-gonna fall down and I have to hold on. I d-don't seem to be able to really let go. And then some things, they j-just seem to p-push me over the edge . . . I dunno, I can't explain it, I j-just know something is crying out inside m-me.'

'Jesus, we're all fucked up to the eyeballs, I guess.'

'Let's not g-go on about it, huh?'

'You feeling funny?'

'J-Just hold me, Mouse, j-just shove those big tits of yours into my f-face and let me d-drown.'

170

'Huh-uh. OK, just this once. But then, Stray my dear, we should start to think positively about what to do. You know, ways to get out of ourselves, ways to get ourselves back.'

*   *   *

Des was thinking about Bertha as he approached his house. She hadn't been in touch. No wounded voice or harsh words. He began to feel that she must be up to something, but couldn't see the angle she might have. Maybe, as Errol had hinted, old ties had been revived. Des knew that he hadn't been all that square with her as an employee. He knew the sex was going to turn things nasty. He suddenly became worried that he would never see his final cheque. But all this quickly became lost to him. The catch was down on the Yale in his front door.

Sweat returned to Des's brow. He looked through his front window. The sofa was upside-down and gutted. He made his way down the side entry and into his back yard. The kitchen door was wide open. His feet crunched glass as he went inside. He found a hammer under the sink, held onto it firmly and then began to look around. The kitchen hadn't been messed with and so he crept forward into his sitting room. Bookshelves had been tipped over, chairs upended and the TV kicked in. Des looked down at a spread of dirt where a plant pot had been toppled. A neat chisel-shaped shoeprint sat in the middle of it. Des let out a weary groan but as he looked around at the chaos, a cold sense of rage began to grow. He edged his way through the mess on the floor, his hammer poised to swing, and started to check out the rest of the house.

The front room was supposed to be his office. Des didn't have much in the way of paperwork, but what there was carpeted the floor in between the broken furniture and flung-away drawers. He saw some of the letters he'd had from Miranda and a lot of photos of the doomed affair, all cast off and trampled by the chisel-toed shoes. The anger grew, ice blue turning hot red as Des clenched the hammer with a surge of vindictiveness. *This wasn't part of the deal. This is too shit close for anyone. This is totally not on!* Des headed for the stairs, fuming with an outrage that impaired his senses. The creak on the landing didn't register. He only raised his head when halfway up. Des didn't have time to react.

With one hand pressed against the wall and the other sliding on the banister, the man with floppy hair launched himself forward feet first. The chisel-shaped shoes thumped Des in the chest. Des got the sight of a peculiar grin and then he was freefalling. A rush of air in his ears. A split-second thought of pain. Then pain became reality. A solid thump into his back and his head whiplashing to the ground with a ferocious crunch. A swirl of noise and light, and a mouth that didn't know how to breathe.

Des, winded and confused, knew the intruder would be coming after him. He flapped around for his hammer, tried to ease himself up but all his strength had gone. The grin was right above him, coming in closer. Des felt knees pinioning his arms and the dead weight of the man sitting on his chest.

'All good things come to an end, eh mate?'

Des thought he was looking at two faces and he could hardly hear the words that sneered down for all the bees that swarmed in his brain.

'That's if your life had any good things in it.'

Des began to consider how he might reply. There was enough abuse in amid the swarm to fill his mouth, but the problem was his mouth wasn't working too well. It was like a broken bellows sucking, gasping and barely processing any air. Above him, Des saw his assailant donning a pair of gloves.

'Thing is, mate, you might just have a chance. You know, get in a few more fucks, a few more nights down the pub . . .'

The gloved hands splayed out in front of Des. They came down slowly, began to cling to his neck, the thumbs smoothing his windpipe.

'All I need to know is where the photos are.'

The man leaned in closer. Des saw a swirl of lines like dancing centipedes on his forehead.

'YOU GOT THAT? THE PHOTOS!' he shouted.

At first, Des wanted to say that he couldn't speak. Ridiculous. The thought doubled his fear and made him strain desperately to get his mouth working.

'F-F-Fuck . . .' was all he could manage.

'You stupid, daft bastard.'

The thumbs began to press down. Des tried to get more words into his mouth but it was like his mouth was no longer there. He looked up and there seemed to be no sign of his attacker. All he could see was what looked like snow. *Snow in late summer? That's something to tell Miranda about. Miranda? Why the hell am I thinking about her at death's door. What about Pearl? Jesus, Miranda, still . . . how bloody deep does it go?*

The snow seemed to be getting heavier and Des became aware of hands pawing over his body as though perhaps he was already dead and the authorities had come to take him away. 'Hold on!' Des screamed to himself. 'Not yet! I've got to come up with a better last thought, you know, something warm and hopeful.' Des struggled. Night seemed to be descending fast. *Fuck words . . . Mere snowflakes falling on a deep-running river . . . huh, now there's something to put in the mouth if I ever find it . . .*

20

There was someone in the other room. Or maybe they were in the same room but far away. Des could hear clumping steps, clattering noises and scrapes. This would be the autopsy. The coroner preparing scalpels, saws and drills ready for dissection. It always had been a thing Des found disgusting and would never wish for, even after death. He tried to move but knew it was impossible. The bastards! Who sanctions such casual butchery? I like my body! I want it going to the grave in one piece! The noises were getting closer, the footsteps and the rattling. Des could hear breathing and then something wet being put on his face. *Jesus! Not the head first, not the rotary skull-opener! They're not going to pull out my brain, are they?* Des felt hands on his shoulders, pulling and shaking; and he thought he heard a voice saying his name. Name? Wasn't he just a number now, a number on a tag on a big toe? More confusion. Des felt hair on his face and thought he could see an eye looking at him, an eye and a mouth saying, 'Des.' Then it all became clear. Bertha.

'Bloody hell, Des, I really thought you were a goner.'

'You – you don't need to . . . do it. I can tell you the cause.' Des was surprised that his mouth was working, sort of, a croaking mouth full of sand, ball-bearings and sounds that may not have been words.

'I'm so glad you've come round,' Bertha said. 'When I

got here, Jesus, what a shock, you were lying stone cold in the hall. I don't know fuck about first aid but I thought I could feel some sort of pulse so then I lugged you onto the sofa.'

'God. I ache everywhere.'

'I was panicking. Thought I should've called an ambulance. You've been out for ages, Des.'

'Guess I'm back now. Still snowing outside, is it?'

'What? Des, have some hot tea, try to move a bit, and tell me who the bastard was who did this!'

The tea helped. It burned and felt weird going down his throat but it gave Des some sense of equilibrium back. He sat up on the sofa, light-headed and wobbly, and looked at Bertha's frowning face.

'I should've been more prepared . . . in more ways than one.' It felt strange speaking, like the ball-bearings were still there, but Des got the hang of it.

'So who was it?'

'I've seen him around. Wild yellowish hair, stocky, had a heavy frown and a sort of sneering face.'

'I think I know who that is.'

'I think I can guess.'

'Scobie Brent, Ross's heavy.'

'That's what I reckoned.'

'God, it makes the connection clear, doesn't it?'

'Seems to.'

'What a bastard!' Bertha looked edgily round the room. 'He's not going to give in easily.'

'Why should he? He's looking at a big fall.'

'So how are you now, Des?'

'Shaky, but OK.'

'You think we should call this whole thing off?'

Des wasn't quite with the situation. There was Bertha, a woman he was vaguely aware he was involved with, but who sat some distance away and looked as nervous as hell.

Shouldn't she be holding him now, giving him comfort and succour? But then Des didn't really want her as he was also vaguely conscious of a river and of a voice calling up from the depths. He didn't know where to focus so tried to stay in work mode; it was impersonal that way.

'We can't call if off now,' he said, wondering whether his words had any expression. 'We're on the threshold of success. We've got the sods panicking.'

'But, Des, it's getting dangerous. Ross'll kill you if you get any nearer.'

'I'll be ready next time, so don't worry about me.'

'I dunno, Des . . .'

Des could now see that Bertha was extremely nervy and that her attitude had changed. No more sensual intrigue or sexy looks. This change urged him to try out some reckless bravado.

'Anyway, I'm near enough ready to bring Ross out into the open, set a trap with the help of the police.'

'Oh no, Des, I don't think that's a good idea.'

'Come on, if you want to nail Claudette's killer, we're going to have to exert pressure.'

'No.' Bertha eased forward and tried to look calm. 'I think maybe we should call it off now. You give me the photos and we'll work out how much cash I owe you.'

It wasn't hard for Des to look stunned. He was stunned, all over, and functioning on automatic pilot. Bertha's words were disturbing, but he couldn't quite grasp why. A sudden sense of thwarted lust and job insecurity swept along the river beneath him and Des shivered.

'I don't believe this. I mean, don't you want to do right by your daughter?'

'Des, don't. Just give me the photos, eh, and we'll talk about the rest later, when you're feeling better.'

'The photos . . .'

She still hadn't looked him in the eye. Des continued to

try to work out Bertha's attitude but then the issue of the photos sank in.

'Well, I've only got one, the other is in a safe place –' He stalled and felt under his shirt. 'Jesus, that's it. That's probably why I'm still here!'

'What is going on, Des?'

'I had one in my shirt. Scobie must've found it and stopped throttling me.'

'God, Des, what's happening? Where's the other one?'

'You'd never guess. But don't worry, I've got lots of copies of both of them ready and waiting.'

'Des, I want them, all of them! Me, I've paid for the lot.'

'You'll get them, Bertha.' Des suddenly began to feel sleepy. 'I've got a few things to sort out, and then we'll settle up – you know, the photos and the money . . .'

The weight on his eyelids was growing heavier and the deep-flowing river was beginning to drown his thoughts.

'Why don't we go to bed?' he heard himself saying. 'It seems like ages since we snuggled up all hot and steamy . . .'

As Bertha looked at him with alarm, Des sank smiling into a deep sleep.

*   *   *

'Me know you, ennit? Didn't we a meet at a New Year's do down at the George?'

'I doubt it very much.'

'Surely we did.'

The guy hovering over Bertha was definitely on his way down. His brown cheeks were lined and his frizzed, thinning hair was tinged with grey. The thing that turned off Bertha the most, though, was his suit – wrinkled, stained and half off his shrunken shoulders.

'I never forget a face and I know I've never met you.'

'Well, would you like a drink anyway?'

'I'd just like to be left alone.'

The guy's pale hazel eyes didn't persevere. Indeed, his whole body language seemed to say he knew he was lost before he began. Another no-hoper going through the motions, Bertha thought. The pub is full of them. Dreams turned sour. Hard-luck stories and tight-lipped bitterness. They're all here propping up the bar. Bertha tried to dispel her observation, but could still feel a sense of desperation. She was part of the scene and it was getting older and scarier. The yearly shrinkage of the horizon to the point where life becomes those few shabby streets you're able to walk down. God – awful!

Bertha picked up her gin and half emptied it. If I can get a few years in on the game through Ross and milk it hard, then, then maybe I will get out, set up my own number and worry no more. Hotel Erotica by the sea. Or perhaps Hotel Claudette for the sexually adventurous. A discreet but popular little establishment. A niche in the market. A potential goldmine.

Bertha stifled a smile. *Don't go too far ahead!* There was McGinlay to get out of the way first. There was Ross to be forced into line. *Why do things always get hard when you see a way out?* She could see but two alternatives. Get Des bumped off and grab the photos. Paddy could well arrange that. Or, get Des back into her bed and sneak the snaps off him. The idea wasn't unpleasant. On the contrary, it was very appealing and that was the problem. He seemed to be able to have his way with her. Bertha picked up her gin and gulped the rest down. 'No blame, girl,' she said to herself. 'You do what you have to.'

* * *

The battered Ford Transit groaned and clunked through the dark streets, leaving a trail of poisonous fumes behind it. Mouse, driving erratically, was with Jerry. Both wore balaclavas and dark sunglasses and were keeping a lookout for street names.

'How you feeling now, Stray?'

'B-Better. You were right about the g-gear. I k-kind of feel safe.'

'That's good. Guess it's like soldiers and stuff who go out on a mission.'

'Yeh, we're on a m-mission.'

'Too right!'

'Shit, is that the r-road there?'

Mouse turned the steering wheel drastically to the right and the old van slewed across the main road and into a tree-lined lane.

'This is where it gets difficult. These fucking country places, you don't know where you are.'

'Ych, it's all t-trees and b-bushes. Urgh, scares the living d-daylights out of me.'

'Don't worry, Stray, we shouldn't need to get out of the van.'

'God, if I wasn't with you . . .'

Many a leafy lane had a dousing of exhaust fumes before the Transit, faded blue and rusty, reached its place of call. Mouse kept the engine running as the two of them inspected the wrought-iron gates.

'Jesus, p-posh eh? You d-don't think p-people actually live like this.'

'That's why they live out here, so you don't see.'

'And this is the b-bastard who g-got M-Mary k-killed! I f-f-f-f . . . shit!'

'Take it easy, Stray. We'll get the sod.'

'B-But how? Look at those g-gates.'

'Hold on tight and I'll show you.'

Mouse suddenly put the van in gear and slammed her foot on the accelerator. With a loud groan, the van lurched forward and then trundled fast straight at the gates. Jerry covered his eyes as they crashed, but the bolt of the gate easily snapped and the van went hurtling through.

'Wow-wee!'

'D-Did you see that?'

'A piece of piss. Now, get ready to slide your door open and we'll give the bastard hell!'

Mouse drove into the forecourt of Sir Martin Wainwright's pile at speed. The headlights of the van had been smashed by the gates so she couldn't see too well. On hitting the gravel, she turned the steering wheel hard, slewing stones all over the place and knocking over a lion rampant by the front steps. Jerry slid open his door. He picked up half-bricks he had under his seat and began to lob them at the windows.

'You b-bastard!' he yelled. 'You murdering scum, we're on to you!'

Mouse opened her door. She brought up a couple of Molotov cocktails she had wedged under her seat. As she fumbled around for her lighter, the front door to the house opened. Two men came cautiously down the steps.

'Stray! Fling a few bricks at those bastards!'

Jerry did. And with relish. He was beginning to feel better than he had for a very long time. His stutter seemed to have left him.

'Here you are, you bastards, get a mouthful of brick!' he shouted as he sent the men into retreat with well-aimed missiles.

Mouse then lit the petrol-soaked cloth in the bottles. She stepped out of the van and sent one bottle through a smashed window. The other she hurled at the front door. The two men dived for cover as the door exploded in flames. A room then burst alive with fire. Mouse saw more people coming from around the back of the house.

'Shit, Stray, it's time to beat it!'

180

Jerry continued picking up bricks from around his feet and chucking them out into the flame-smeared night, relishing the articulation of unhindered expletives. Mouse, meanwhile, got back in the van. She grated into reverse, then swung round and back into the darkness of the drive. As the van disappeared from view, a group of shocked people heard a singsong of swearwords piercing the cool night air.

*   *   *

There was a question as to where Des was. Yes, he was sitting in the snug of the George pub, but he wasn't exactly sure that the pub was real. Or maybe he wasn't real? Des looked at the bland walls and shivered. Whatever, he thought, I'm sure this is just a temporary dislocation. He looked down at his whisky. It appeared to wink. Jesus . . . In the circumstances, it would've been better if Des had been allowed to sleep, but the phone had ruined all that. First of all, Liam had rang and told him the prints were ready. And then Pearl had come on the line and a woozy Des had suddenly found himself turned liquid with emotion. He was practically sobbing to her with a frog-filled voice about how the river was flowing away and time was running out.

'We can't let the moment slip,' he rambled on to her.

Pearl had sounded concerned, both about his sanity and his sentiments, and it was not without some reservation that she agreed to meet him. But since then Des had felt a little more composed. He managed to pick up the prints from Liam, who seemed pretty anxious to be shot of the situation. Des then went back and stashed the photos under his carpet in various places. The obvious can often be the best, he felt. It was all very smooth, very professional, but then, once in the pub, faced with the prospect of Pearl . . .

181

She came in wearing a black astrakhan overcoat. Her face and hair positively glowed with the contrast. After drinks were sorted out, she sat down opposite Des and gave him a worried inspection. Des knew it was incumbent on him to explain and he did so in a detached, matter-of-fact way. The words came out calmly enough, but inside Des felt he was riding waves. One second Pearl was a vision seen through whisky, the next she was far away and looking vexed.

'You should be in bed, Des, you look dreadful.'

'I know, but I didn't want to miss you.'

'This isn't good.'

'We both know about our shitty jobs.'

'But we were avoiding that, and now look what's happened.'

'I'll be fine tomorrow.'

Pearl looked as if she was going to say more, but she pulled back and made her mouth small. She shook her head at Des and gave off a tight smile.

'It is good to see you. A bright light in a lousy day.'

Des felt that his mouth was working well, but was conscious that maybe the language of the rest of his body didn't quite match his words. Certainly Pearl seemed cautious as though expecting him to keel over or freak out at any minute.

'I'm all right,' Des insisted.

'Like fuck you are. I think you're still in shock.'

'Yeh. Guess I am still a bit wobbly.'

'We shouldn't have had this meeting. It's messing up the magic we had, it's making me doubt the situation.'

'You could always take me in hand.'

'I'll take you home, Des, that's all.'

'Good enough, I guess.'

'But, Des, this worries me. It's depressing. The shit, we both have it but it shouldn't come between us. It shouldn't be here now.'

'Guess it's bound to happen.'

'No, and if it does, well it's just like the rest of the shit, no difference.'

'I didn't exactly plan to be strangled.'

'I know, you daft bastard. Let's leave it for now and I'll take you home.'

Des made the most of her smile before he thought of his house and the trashed up mess he was going to have to recuperate in.

21

There was a shaft of sunlight in the bedroom. As Des opened his eyes, he saw it catch an upended vase and sparkle. Des smiled. All was quiet; his body felt rested and refreshed. Yesterday was a bad dream departed. Des squirmed around under the duvet, thought of staying put and leaving the clearing up of his house till later. He tried to focus his thoughts on Pearl, but then the cold mechanical tones of the phone interrupted him. An irritated hand flopped over.

'Yeh.' Des found it hard to say it and the word came out as a croak.

'McGinlay! This is the last straw! I'm going to break you, you bastard, and your pathetic little life!'

Des swallowed phlegm to try to ease his throat. He needed a coffee, a fag and not a phone call. 'Who's the fan?' he managed to say.

'You know full well and you know that today your time has run out!'

'It ran out yesterday, mate, but I got a second chance.' His throat was easing.

'Are you on something? I guess I should expect it.'

'Who is this?'

'Wainwright! The one whose house you arranged to be attacked. I'm sure it was you. You're just the sort of low-life who'd get yobs to throw bricks and petrol bombs!'

'Sir Martin, I don't know what the fuck you're talking about.'

'I expected you to say that. However, regardless of denials, McGinlay, today is your nemesis, so expect a call. Only the photos can save you now.'

'So what's the cash offer?'

'That deal's off.'

'Huh-uh. Well you'd better go fuck yourself then.'

The coffee went down like molten metal but it did the trick. Despite some soreness, Des decided he was almost one hundred per cent. He picked up a chair in his living room and looked down at the chisel-shaped shoeprint. One job among many. As Des surveyed the mess of his house, he knew it was time for decisiveness. The world was closing in and he had to make some moves. He stood up abruptly and picked up the phone.

'Hi, it's Des. You still talking to me?'

'Dunno, depends on what you've got to say.'

'Well, Errol, I reckon it's time for some co-operation.'

'Ah. You do, huh? That's very nice of you, Des. I mean, I feel so honoured.'

'Yeh, yeh. I've been an arsehole.'

'Huh, tell me something I don't know.'

'Well, I got throttled three-quarters to death by Scobie Brent yesterday and Sir Martin Wainwright's promising to finish the job today.'

'The situation is becoming clear. You're in deep shit and you want help.'

'I wouldn't put it quite like –'

'An now you got the cheek to come runnin to me after holdin out on me for days.'

'I guess I'd have to say I'm sorry about that.'

'Wow, such contrition! The power of fear!'

'What was that word again?'

'What's on your mind, Des?'

'Some kind of set-up, Errol. I was thinking, all these shits, they want to deal. So why don't I make one? Photos for cash and information; a hidden mike up my sleeve.'

'Who you got in mind?'

'Constanza, I reckon. Scobie Brent probably did all the dirty work but Constanza must've given the orders to protect his smarmy client. He can shop them both.'

'I dunno, man. You've gotta be careful about such set-ups, entrapment and the like. Then there's the question of what my bosses'll think of me using a dickhead like you.'

'Come on. It's bona fide undercover work. And even if it is inadmissible, it could provide the basis for action, like giving Scobie a forensic once-over.'

'Yeh, there could be mileage in that.'

'You up for it then?'

'Give me a few hours.'

'Right, and I'll get some of those snaps over to you.'

'Did you really nearly get snuffed?'

'I saw the river, man.'

'Jeez, you are a mad bastard.'

After putting the phone down, Des began to sort out the mess that surrounded him. It was a highly motivational activity. Each item righted provided a cause for what he wanted to do next. He sorted out most of everything as best he could, leaving only the footprint on the carpet and the hammer lying by the front door.

*　　*　　*

'I'm not happy, Bertha. I don't like this. There's too many ifs and buts. Really, to be honest, it all seems half-cocked.'

'Come on, Paddy, you can't expect things to be written down in black and white. What is in this line of business?'

'If it's run as an escort agency, then most of it can be legit, just like the saunas.'

'We can make it that way. Ross, he just likes playing the role of pimp to the rich.'

'I don't know. I'm getting old, I like things clean and straight. I'm hooked on security these days.'

Paddy Conroy's Mercedes was parked on Vyse Street. This gave him and Bertha a view of an old graveyard where the soot-blackened tombs and defaced angels of Victorian high society still stood. Paddy was paranoid about meeting Bertha in anything other than the most austere circumstances. He justified this on the basis that he 'still wasn't sure about her', but really he knew that, even now, she could charm his trousers down and that was another risk too far.

'Look, Paddy, you don't have to fret about these things. We'll set up a legit agency and I'll filter out all the contacts I get from Ross; anything dodgy, I'll handle that personally.'

'There's the thing, can you trust Ross?'

'Once the deal is set up, then yes. I was surprised when I saw him. Still a revolting bastard, but he seemed tired, maybe even glad to get a few things off his hands.'

'I can't believe that.'

'No, really. The photos he said would put him sweet with Wainwright and some deals they've got planned.'

'You can't trust the man.'

'There is a problem, though.'

'One among many I'm sure.'

'Des, this private investigator I've got working for me, I reckon he's got too involved. He's talking about getting the police in.'

'I told you, Bertha, didn't I? I told you this thing was half-cocked.'

'Don't worry, Paddy. We can handle this.'

'I would've thought you'd've had him round your little finger.'

'Yeh, well I thought I had, and I still hope I can get him in line because he's got the photos and I need those in our deal with Ross.'

Paddy stared at a nearby stone Jesus, arms once raised to the heavens but now lopped off, and he groaned inwardly. Put her off, he thought. String things along to the very last and hope that she screws up.

'That's the first job then, isn't it, Bertha, before we can do else all,' he said. 'What's the point in tackling Ross until you've got the leverage?'

'I think I can swing it, but as a standby, Paddy, we might need some of your doormen.'

'Bertha, I told you, I'm not happy with this kind of thing!'

Bertha leaned over and put a hand on Paddy's thigh. She smiled, one of those smiles that dispel age and bring back memories. Paddy tried to keep his eye on the armless Christ.

'Come on, Paddy, don't be a daft sod, it's just a fall-back, I'm not asking you to rub the guy out.'

*   *   *

The sun was a red balloon caught on the steel gantry of a container crane. The crane, normally yellow, had burned black and it cast a shadow right over to where Des was standing. The days were drawing in. A foreground and forethought of a colder darkness, pale pinks and violet receding to the horizon of someone else's summer. Des shivered. The idea was alarming. He looked away from the pastel fires of the sky and concentrated on the road that stretched before him. From the phone call he'd made he'd learned that Scobie would come in around seven. There was no suspicion from the guy who answered the phone, to him it was just a call from a crony down the Lime who owed a few quid. Des was propping up a wall at the side of

Conference Cars and making a fag-end carpet. He'd already sussed that Ross was still inside. A prospect of decisive times, if only the sneering shit with the floppy hair would come.

He finally did. A souped-up VW noisily entered the car park and revved to a halt in front of a clump of litter-strewn berberis. Scobie smoothed his hair in the rear-view mirror and then got out. He whistled tunelessly as he jauntily bounced on ridiculous trainers up the showroom steps. The sun had dipped below the container depot now, so Des could easily move though shadow and catch Scobie by surprise.

The first hammer blow went straight on his nose. A short, sharp thud, a snapping sound and a sudden burst of blood. Scobie staggered back and teetered on the top step. Des kicked him in the groin and Scobie went tumbling down. He was on his hands and knees by the time Des had descended the steps. Another hammer blow to the head sent him sprawling onto his back. Des stooped and grabbed the thick straw hair. He used it to pull Scobie over to the shrubbery, then turned his head and pushed his face into the dark soil. Scobie was soon choking for air and Des let him do so for quite some time. Then he let the head go and Scobie turned, gulping, his face a mess of blood and dirt. Des didn't say anything. He saw his enemy's eyes register recognition and then he put his foot on Scobie's windpipe. He pressed down, ground his shoe hard until Scobie writhed and gurgled helplessly. His tongue began to loll out, his blood splattered crisp packets and old condoms, and turned the berberis prematurely red. Des nearly didn't stop, but another idea came to him. In turn, Des pinioned both hands and hammered Scobie's fingers ferociously.

The beneficial effects were immediate. A mighty load had been lifted from his shoulders and a slab of frustration expelled. Des sighed with relief. Leaving Scobie groaning, he stepped up to the front doors of Conference Cars and pushed them open. He headed straight for the office, giving the cars a good thwack with his hammer as he passed them. Gus hardly had time to see what was happening. A sudden thrust in his gut from the hammer and then Des had him in an arm-lock, bundling him forward into Ross's presence.

'What the fuckin hell –?'

Des pushed Gus's face onto the desk and then pulled his arm well back behind him. He gave Ross a heavy glare.

'I'm a very angry man, Constanza. I've had it up to here with your shit and it's got to be sorted!'

'Jesus. OK, OK, calm down.'

Ross had his hands up in alarm and it was then that Des saw the missing finger. He thought he should've known that before, but he couldn't be bothered to work out why he didn't.

'I'm going to let the geezer go, OK, and we're going to have a quiet chat, OK, about Wainwright and his randy ways. No fuckery, OK?'

'So you're McGinlay, eh? All right, we've no need for aggravation right at this moment. It's business, right?'

Des eased up on the arm-lock and pushed Gus away from him. There were oceans of silent fury in Gus's eyes, but a look from Ross kept the hate locked in. Gus propped up the wall as Des sat down in front of the desk.

Ross became quite conciliatory when Des told him of Scobie's attack.

'I have to say I am sorry, mate, that guy is out of control. He never bloody does what I tell him to. "No aggro," I said to him. "Do a deal, steal em if you must, but no aggro." I'm glad you told me about it, really. The guy has just got to go. He's a real liability.'

'Well he won't be doing much for a while.'

190

'What? You clobbered him?'

'He's grovelling in dog turds outside right now.'

'Bloody hell, that must be the first time Scobie's got done. Jesus Christ, you've done me a favour, mate.'

'I'm glad we've got something going, because perhaps now we can do a deal.'

'A deal?'

Des reached inside his coat pocket, pulled out some copy prints and threw them on the desk. 'I've got lots of these, dozens, hidden all over the place, and the negatives . . . still as embarrassing as ever.'

'So, Scobie, the wanker, got fuck all?'

'Looks like the lot of you have been one step off the pace all along.'

Ross Constanza had sagged. He lit up a cigarette fussily and kept his eyes well down. His brow had become stretch-marked with thought.

'Shit,' he said to no one in particular before he looked up at Des. 'OK, you'd better tell me what you've got in mind,' he began. 'But no promises, right? I've got others to consult. OK? So let's have it.'

Just two final tasks. Des smiled, but was conscious it was an uneasy one. He carefully washed his hammer under the tap and then got a dustpan to remove the chisel-shaped footprint. That's when the uneasiness grew. Did he really do that, and enjoy it? Did he really barge in on Constanza without a second thought? Des shivered involuntarily and a sheen of sweat suddenly flushed his brow. Jesus! How could I? He almost slumped down in delayed shock and might well have done if the phone hadn't rung. Its cold tones sounded welcoming.

'Hi there, Desmond. This is Miranda here.'

'Y-Yeh?'

Another shock, and from a really unexpected direction.

Des began to flounder. The floor was turning liquid again.

'I hope you don't mind me ringing. I know I really shouldn't but – well, I was somewhat worried.'

Des felt utterly speechless.

'You still there?'

'Y-Yeh, guess so.'

'It's that note, Des, and the photo. It just seemed like you were in deep trouble.'

'You mean you care about it?'

'Of course I care. Whatever our conflicts, whatever the way we are now, we did have some good times and you still mean something to me.'

'Could've fooled me.'

'Come on, Des, don't start. You do know what I mean and you do know why I've been the way I have.'

'Maybe I haven't had time to think about that.'

'Are you OK? You're not in some awful danger, are you?'

'I'm as fine as I can be under the circumstances.' Des almost added, 'And no thanks to you,' but then realized he didn't quite feel that way. 'The photo, it was just insurance that's all, like you're always forking out for but rarely ever need.'

'That makes me feel better.'

Des remained silent.

'Let's not say any more, yeh? I'll see you around some time?'

'Yeh, guess so,' he said.

Des put the phone down. He looked at his TV set with its kicked in screen. He smiled. Shit, I'm not angry, he thought. Pretty well unmoved . . . Des leaned forward as if watching a programme. Yeh, and the telly's better this way. He laughed. He hadn't done that in a long time.

22

The deal was set. Errol rang Des, Des rang Ross and a meet was fixed for the following day. Then it was pay cheque time. And Des could sit back and think about love. In fact, he was already thinking about love, sitting outside the Waterside Café and waiting for Pearl. Love, some sandy beach and those wispy trees. A new horizon presenting itself, though feebly perceived amid the brick walls and dank canal that surrounded him. But then, Des had an uncomfortable thought: shoulders drooping and the winter coming, what was a few weeks in the wide-open blue but a frustrating distraction? Shit, stuff that down the back of the sofa!

He lit a fag and watched Pearl coming over the old iron bridge. They waved. She wore shades and a thigh-length yellow dress that head-turned city suits, making them bump into each other.

Hell, Pearl herself was a beach down by the dark waters – sunshine on sand and strands of golden kelp. Maybe Des could afford to raise his head a few inches?

'You're looking pretty stunning, Pearl.'

'Yeh, turn a few heads down the meat market, fetch a good price.'

'Well, that's nice.'

'You weren't feeling romantic, were you?'

'Yeh, actually I was. I was thinking about Madeira or the

Canary Isles, like the splash of yellow you are in this dismal place.'

'Working clothes, Des, and I've just had a lousy day.'

'Looks like I'm going to join you.'

'Sorry, hon. A couple of really fat punters and Carlos giving me shit for being rude and I've just had it.'

'We were supposed to be keeping all that stuff separate.'

'Guess it's not working, huh?'

Pearl frowned and began to chew a nail. Des stared at the murky water. *I reckon I'm getting this. Sod expectation, just go with the flow, no matter how sordid it gets. One working philosophy for a city dick . . .*

'I should've asked, shouldn't I? How're you feeling today?'

'So much goes on in between . . . I'm feeling OK, Pearl, much better, but now it's you who's down in the dumps, what can you do?'

'I'm going to have to split the scene, Des. I can't take much more of this. I need a complete fresh start.'

'A beach mid-Atlantic? I should have the money tomorrow.'

'A tempting thought, but first, Des, food. Shit, I'm hungry as hell.' Pearl smiled for the first time. 'If we don't move soon, I'm gonna take a bite out of your big thigh.'

'Feel free, sweetheart, and I'll do the same to yours. Who needs a restaurant?'

'Not a fair deal, Des, your tough old meat for my sweet butt.'

Bad feeling dispelled, Des and Pearl went off to eat. French-style this time, in among business people confidently blathering golf and good wine. A couple of misfits making dreams amid furtive stares and feared-for wallets. And Des glowered on cue while Pearl pouted and they both fondled hands, seeking out the exact fantasy that would set them free.

'I could go back to cab-driving.'

'I've got to get off the game, Des, and there's no way you could afford to keep me.'

'There must be a respectable end to what I do, good rates and clean work.'

'I need a good business angle. I was thinking of interior design.'

'Wouldn't we be able to think better in Las Palmas?'

'You just want to get my knickers down.'

'That, and all those defences.'

'Don't say that, Des, it scares me.'

'Huh? Ah, go with the flow, right?'

'Don't you have any other skills you could sell, Des?'

'Loads, but I haven't found them yet.'

'I still think we might have a nice time finding them.'

'Now that does cheer me up.'

'Good, because I'll have to go soon. Second shift; Carlos calls.'

'Oh no . . .'

'You mean you've got no calls on you?'

'Just a murder to wrap up.'

'Ha, you should shout that out loud –'

Des began to look around the restaurant.

'– But don't bother, huh. The way it goes for both of us, but I think we're on the right path.'

'I can see the plane taking off in the distance.'

'And maybe just . . .'

'We two?'

Go with the flow. Des was doing just that, driving somewhere south-east of the city, a place he didn't know, looking for Jerry Coton. He felt good, like he'd found the groove he wanted and that life was on the up. But there was a niggling uneasiness. Go with the flow. Fine, but what if it was sewer-bound? Claudette, she probably felt the same as

Des when she got her hook on Wainwright, moving forward and a view beyond what she could see. Now Des was closing in on her fate and expecting the same payday. The same outcome? Des shivered. He'd just checked out old grey Frederick and found out about the squat.

'Watch out dere, man,' the old geezer had said. 'Dat bwoy im goin right over the edge.'

Frederick's words suddenly jarred, as though they could apply to anyone, especially to Des. He turned the car into Anselm Road and cruised down looking at house numbers. 'Sod it,' he groaned. 'Whatever. Any number of nasty things could crop up, Jerry Coton for one.'

'This is some shit heap of a place you've got here, Jerry.'

'I d-dunno if I w-want to see you.'

'Not much choice now.'

'I'm m-making a n-new start.'

'Yeh . . .'

Des looked around at the sparse room. A mattress on the floor, an armchair and a few piles of books. Jerry was lying sulkily on the bed smoking ganja.

'Not even the first rung of the ladder.'

'Who c-cares?'

'Sounds like the spliff talking.'

'What do you want, M-McGinlay?'

'You trashed Wainwright's pile, didn't you, you stupid arsehole? And the pompous toad is blaming me, threatening all kinds of retribution.'

'I had t-to do something, that's all, and he d-deserves it, and m-more!'

'Maybe, but you should keep well out of it. You're just an ant he wouldn't even notice squashing.'

'He's g-got to p-pay, McGinlay. He c-can't get away with it!'

'It's being arranged, OK? We're setting up a bit of a scam

tomorrow night with the heavies that did it, and what we get out of that should nail Wainwright. So no more fuckery, Jerry. Just smoke your weed, feel sorry for yourself and go with the flow. I tell you, the world'll open up again in a few months time.'

'Wow. M-Mr Optimist.'

'Two sides of the coin. You look up or you look down. The rest is bollocks.'

'Oh, M-Mr Cynic now?'

'Don't mind me, Jerry.'

Des suddenly noticed the pale square of the picture frame on the wall. He went over to look at it. 'That is spooky,' he said. 'You should give the room a lick of paint.'

'It's a self-portrait.'

'God . . . Jerry . . . wanker.'

The next meeting was a car park job, back of a burger bar; Des's rusty Lancia next to the sleek Audi in which a cautious Errol smiled. He had come up trumps. The wire and Des were official. Any ploy to nobble Ross Constanza was acceptable to the powers that be. He hadn't, however, dared mention Wainwright, thinking that would make things political and so scupper proceedings. Awkward for Errol when Des handed over a couple of the notorious prints.

'Shit, it'd be better if this comes out through Ross. Covers us, yeh?'

'Well, I don't care, Errol.'

'You don't have a boss who plays golf with his knighthood.'

'That bad, eh?'

'Wouldn't surprise me if they were secret lovers too.'

'Now that would be a story . . .'

Sitting separate in the two cars, they began to talk through the arrangements for the meet. Errol was still being cagey, but he was on board and Des felt better because of it. He needed the support. His next job was to see Bertha. Tricky situation.

A big smile greeted Des when she opened the door. A big smile from a made-up face and a welcoming body wrapped loosely in pink silk. Des heard a bell ring in his head and he didn't know what he was going to do about it.

'I was sort of expecting you,' she said.

'Well, we've got things to sort out.'

'You're looking much better, Des.'

'When it gets very bad, bad itself can seem good, if you know what I mean.'

'Yeh. Until you see what good's like.'

They sat down on the sofa in the room of pink frills, Bertha's dressing gown already slipping off smooth curves and Des beginning to find it hard to think. He fixed his eyes on her reflection in the blank television screen. It seemed to help.

'So you still want to call it off?'

'I think it would be the best thing.'

'What kind of deal are you making, Bertha?'

'I'm thinking of yours and my safety. The job's done now. We more or less know the truth and if we push it further – the stakes are too high for them, they'll just murder again.'

'Sounds like bullshit to me. You said you wanted to nail Claudette's killer.'

'That was just angry grief talking.'

'Have you actually spoken to Ross?'

'No, of course not.'

'So what d'you want the photos for?'

'To burn them all. It's one memory of my daughter I don't want hanging around and it stops any trouble in its tracks.'

Des knew that Bertha was lying but it didn't seem to

matter any more. He'd set his trap and she didn't need to know a thing about it. In fact, she probably shouldn't know, because Des felt that it wasn't beyond Bertha to have done a deal with Ross. Whatever the situation, she had an angle and that was as plain as the bare thigh that rubbed against his. But did he really know for sure? Why the antagonism, when before he'd felt sorry for the tough deal Bertha had had? Des ventured a look straight in her face. She smiled. Brown eyes glinted. Maybe he did owe her more charitable thoughts. Bertha had brought succour when Des was low down. Motives, ambivalent always. Des eased back and pushed his shoulder against hers. Well, here comes another dodgy motive, he thought.

'You'll drop the case then?'

'As best I can. There are things in motion that might come back to me.'

'But you'll call off the police?'

'You'll be the one with the cards.'

'That's fair enough. I've paid for them.'

Des stared up at the rose-patterned lampshade. She was holding his hand now, stroking the fine hairs on the backs of his fingers. Two sets of total lies locked together and a prospect of the false deals being sealed by sex.

'So what do we do now?'

'What would you like to do?' she asked.

Bertha was massaging his hand, leaning forward and revealing her nakedness beneath the gown. Its power had not diminished in Des's eyes.

'Tomorrow will probably be the last time we meet,' Bertha said. 'After that, it would probably be best to keep our distance for a while.'

'I guess you're right.'

'I'll miss you, Des.'

'Uh-huh.'

'You don't know how to leave, do you?'

'No.'

Bertha straightened herself up next to Des and let the pink gown slip completely off her shoulders. 'Then you'll just have to stay.'

＊   ＊   ＊

It was midnight and Ross Constanza was still in his office. A half-empty bottle of whisky sat on the desk, as did Gus's feet, who was lounging opposite. The striplight in the ceiling had developed a flicker and it was beginning to annoy Ross.

'Fucking first chance to get away, Jesus, man, I'm off – bleedin shit heap! I used to think you should never stay in the same place too long. I let that slip. I can feel the moss growing all over me.'

'Tek it easy, boss. When you see a way out, den tings, dey can seem panicky.'

'I don't know that I do see a way out. I mean, what d'you make of it? A phone call this afternoon from McGinlay saying he wants to do a deal on the photos, and now the same bleedin call from Bertha.'

'The photos dem're like breedin rabbit.'

'Too right. Sounds like the whole world's got them cept us. Hardly seems any point getting them back.'

'What Wainwright im say?'

'He's a pretty angry fucker. Says don't do any deals, just pull out a gatt and take the stuff.'

'Should work wid Bertha, but wid McGinlay . . .'

'Pity he crocked up Scobie.'

'I can handle a gun, man, don' worry.'

'That ain't the worry; it's the fucking tricks he might have up his sleeve.'

'What do dey call dat der ting, man? You know, mekkin the bes out of a lousy situation.'

'Damage limitation.'

'Dat's the fucker.'

'Yeh, well, that's all I've been doing since Wainwright had his "unprotected" sex.'

'Bes ting be to blow im away.'

'Don't think I haven't thought about it, the pompous prick. Never trust a bent straight, Gus. They've got fingers all over the place. You never know where you are.'

'So what's the plan den, Ross?'

'Damage bleedin limitation. We rip off the snaps from Bertha and McGinlay and bung em down Wainwright's throat. End of relationship. Then we bugger off down Waterloo and by dawn we should be supping Pernod by the Seine.'

'Soun's cool.'

'Yeh, just a case of keeping our distance till we see what happens.'

'Fine. Me hear dem say French chicks get pretty hot for guys like me.'

Ross poured himself another drink of whisky. He looked at the soles of Gus's shoes and then at the small office. Too long in one place.

'Gus, take your stinking shoes off my desk! And while you're at it, why don't you fix that fucking light?'

23

Des got almost sentimental about the big wallow. It maybe wasn't so bad to drown your sorrows and soak in self-pity. Those sleepless nights under low lights riding great monologues of thought. Boozy, smoke-filled dawns where the clarity of light was impossible to believe, as though he'd reached an hallucinatory state. It all seemed so cosy and safe compared to the fraught actions he was caught up in now. And the psychology was there, just like the reluctant worker who can't leave his bed. *Things'll go on with out me. What does it matter anyway?* Des was tired. He dragged himself around his house collecting the many copies of photos he was about to do deals with. In some way, he felt the case was over, and the dangerous business of wrapping things up was a burden he didn't have the heart for.

Think of the pay. Think of never seeing Bertha again. Think of Pearl and Las Palmas in the fall . . . Des suddenly felt a twinge of guilt. *No, don't think, don't think at all!*

Three envelopes eventually piled up on Des's kitchen table. For Ross, half a dozen snaps and half the negs. The same for Bertha. The third envelope was a bloody-minded whim. A little sequence which made a story to be sent to the local paper. A felt-tip note: 'Sir Martin Wainwright.' An equals sign. One of the snapshots. Another equals sign and then a press cutting about Claudette's murder. *What the hell?* Des put a stamp on it and then went out of the house to the post box which sat collecting smog on Argent Street. On his way back, Des saw the guy sitting in his car. It was fifty-fifty, of course, that the man was just waiting for someone. However, guys sitting in cars have to be regarded as dodgy. Social Security snooper, debt collector or someone keeping an eye on Des. There'd be but one way to find out.

The first place he had to visit was Bertha's pad. Bitter-sweet, this. A tangle, a badly snagged knot of string that might take a long time to unravel. Des got into his Lancia and set off for the permanent crawl of Argent Street. The guy sitting in his car didn't move but a flashing indicator showed that he was about to. As Des was let into the traffic flow, the car pulled out, a Japanese job, grey and anonymous. The attention was unwelcome. According to Hollywood, Des would now zoom off, jump a few lights and screech around near-impossible turns. Des looked at the long line of traffic. Maximum speed ten yards a minute. Great. He looked back and could see his tail slotting into the flow some five cars back. So who was he working for? Ross? The police? It seemed to Des that this was an element in the situation he did not need, an element that could jeopardize his pay cheque or even his health. He began to feel annoyed, partly at being tailed and partly because of the moronic pace of the traffic. Des stopped his car completely and jolted the handbrake on. Tension was wrapping iron bars around his head. He got out and walked back to the Jap job. The guy sitting in his car had the window down.

'You're violating my rights.'

'Eh, I'm just –'

'I'm not in the mood for being followed. I'm very fussy about my personal space.'

Horns from the stalled cars around them began to blow.

A few irate heads appeared from behind windscreens and standard motoring oaths added to the cacophony. Des reached into the car and grabbed the ignition key.

'Hey! Come here you!'

'Who you working for, huh?'

'Give me those bloody keys and get out of here!'

Des dangled the keys high in the air. He saw a burly builder-type hauling himself out of the car behind, his face contorted with rage.

'We're about to have a major scene. You going to tell me?'

'Shit! All right, I'm doing it for Wainwright. I'm just supposed to make sure you do the deal with Constanza and no funny business. If you do that you're in the clear and you don't have to worry about me.'

'What the bloody hell are you lot doing blocking the fucking road?'

The irate builder was but a few yards away and he had a tyre iron in his hand. Des looked down at the guy sitting in his car.

'Oh well, the way it goes . . .' Then he threw the keys across the road and dashed back to his own car. The noise behind him was growing, the builder had his head in the Jap job, but Des suddenly had an open road in front of him. He got his car going and put his foot down. A few red lights to cross, a few impossible turns to try . . .

*   *   *

'The end of the road then, Bertha?'

'You sure this is all there is? There's not many negatives.'

'They're copy negs. There are only two prints to make copies of.'

'I suppose I should settle up, then.'

'I reckon you should.'

Bertha was dressed up for the occasion. Full make-up

204

that brought back former glories and a dark red dress that shimmered across her ample curves. Des took one look down her cleavage and felt an unwanted surge of desire. One of those places, an old pleasure haunt he was seeking to move on from. Bertha began to count out the money.

'You're sure this is the end of the line for you, Des?'

'From now on I'll refer all queries to you.'

'I don't like the sound of that.'

'Loose ends, Bertha, like Wainwright pressuring me.'

'Doing it my way will stop everything.'

'I hope you're making a good deal, my dear.'

'One day I'll tell you all about it.'

Des sat back on the plum red sofa and allowed himself a sigh of relief. A major job done. A real wad of cash. Las Palmas in his pocket. He could just pack it in and let things go on without him. He could, but he knew he wouldn't. He fingered his throat, a throat that had known the same hands as Claudette and Mary. He had to see it through.

'I'm going to miss you, Des.'

Bertha was leaning towards him and she had her hand on his thigh. A familiar pose this one and, despite himself, Des began to feel rumblings of desire.

'You always do it, don't you, Bertha? Go right down to base instincts.'

'Come on, that's in your mind, and you love it.'

'As if you make sure the thoughts don't arise.'

'Men, Des, you're all the same. It wouldn't matter what I did.'

'Well, you certainly have the chemistry.'

'So, will you miss me?'

'Like wild nights on the town.'

'What's that supposed to mean?'

'You know, it was great while it was happening, but the mornings-after were hard to deal with.'

'Well that's nice.'

Des shrugged. He braced himself for flak.

'Sex and business. That's about as far as it goes for men. The rest is just hassle, to be evaded or shrugged off.'

'I don't know as you're any better.'

'You never dared come close enough to find out.'

'Look, you've paid me off, Bertha, so there's no point in rowing. But if you want to play the who-used-who? game, then I reckon you're ahead and just about to cross the finishing line.'

'Yes? Well, maybe I am about to do that.'

'It'll end in tears.'

'That's what soft shits like you like to think.'

Des was feeling pretty strange when he left Bertha's block of flats. He didn't really want to leave but wanted to return, call Bertha all the names under the sun and then make fierce love to her. It made him unwary. He didn't notice the blue van that was parked some way behind his own car. It had been there before but he hadn't noticed it then because of the Japanese job. Previously, the van had been up ahead of him on Argent Street and had since kept on his tail. He was more concerned now with easing Bertha from his thoughts, and as he set off of to meet Errol, the van barely registered. Des headed for the city centre, working through the crawling traffic and then onto the fast-moving expressway. He swept up Camp Hill, past the stone canyon vista of the city and on. He didn't notice any of it. No panoramas, no horizon, just a blinkered route from an unsettling Bertha to an unknown scene where danger lurked. He got to the glasshouse facade of the railway station feeling calm enough, though a sense of seediness still lingered, old sweat needing to be showered off.

'You're late as usual, Des.'

'Yeh, just been disentangling myself from my employer.'

'You never really told me how entangled you were.'

'Later, eh, Errol, it doesn't bear thinking about just now.'

'The things you get into.'

'The main thing is, I got my cash.'

'Right, let's wrap it up then.'

Des and Errol sat in the front of the unmarked black van and surveyed the meeting place. Three looming tower-blocks encircled the space in front of the station where one broad main road fed into a large roundabout which in turn led to the expressway out of the city. The traffic was constant and busy. A slip road from the main road to the station was where the meeting was planned.

'Whose idea was this?'

'Constanza's. Said he likes railway stations. Said they're a good reminder that you should never stay still too long.'

'He's probably right about that.'

'Yeh. I reckon he knows he's stayed still too long and got his feet stuck. Bumping off whores is a sign of desperation. So, how you reckon it'll be for the meet?'

'It's OK. Lots of people coming and going, cars and vans parked around so we don't look suspicious. Bit of a problem maybe with the traffic noise.'

'I hope I can pull it off.'

'Getting nervy, huh?'

'Yeh. When you see the end of something, you can't help feeling that some unforeseen snag will crop up.'

'By the way, you wouldn't happen to know, would you, how Scobie Brent ended up in the hospital?'

'Me? Nah . . . but it sounds like good news.'

'He's in bad shape apparently, concussion and stuff. We asked the doctors to keep him in as long as possible and we've got a plain clothes guy there keeping an eye on him.'

'So he needs fingering soon?'

'Yeh. And apparently he was half throttled as well. Didn't he do that to you?'

'Yeh, that's another thing doesn't bear thinking about.'

*   *   *

'So what are we g-going to d-do then, Mouse?'

'Dunno, we'll have to work something out.'

'We ought to have a g-gun, that would be b-best.'

'It's good, though, isn't it, what we're doing?'

'G-Guess so.'

'I mean, "revenge", we're actually going to try and do it.'

'Yeh . . .'

'It's got to be one of the biggest repressions around, you know, and that's the way the system wants it. Your mother gets beat up on, your girlfriend gets killed and you're supposed to sit meekly back and let some officious arsehole bring the culprit to justice. Huh! All justice is is punishment by boredom in the nick.'

'And the v-victim's friends or relatives b-bleed slowly to d-death inside.'

'Right, when they should be getting it out of themselves and wreaking their own bloody justice. Of course, we can't have that. People might start bumping off their neighbours. They might start attacking the bastard system itself! God knows, there's enough to seek revenge for there!'

'Too b-bloody right, Mouse.'

'It's starting to get dark.'

'Yeh, c-can't be long now.'

'The dark'll suit us, Stray.'

The battered blue van was parked on the opposite side of the station entrance from Errol's van. A bank of shrubbery obscured most of it from view. Jerry began to roll up a spliff on his knees as he sat in the front passenger seat.

'It must be strange, though, Stray, to know a woman you've been to bed with is dead,' Mouse said.

'W-What d'you mean?'

'Dunno, it just seems odd, creepy even, that you've been really physically intimate with someone, and now that

208

body's lying six feet under being caressed by worms.'

'Jesus, M-Mouse!'

'Haven't you ever thought of it like that?'

'N-No. I think back to when we made love, b-but it's the f-feeling of the moment, the f-feelings about her I m-miss.'

'Must be my warped mind. It does bring home the finality of death, though, the physical awareness of sex suddenly turned to putrefaction.'

'C-Can't you think of anything else to t-talk about?'

'Well, yeh, this is a great spliff.'

'D-Don't I always make em?'

'Mind you, this makes me think of sex too, or feel it more like.'

'What is it n-now?'

'I'm getting horny, Stray.'

'N-Now? I mean we've go-got –'

'Let's go in the back of the van and lie on the mattress,' she suggested.

'What about the m-meeting out there?'

'It could be ages, and I want you to shag me, Stray. And note when I say "you shag me".'

'Eh? I d-don't –'

'You know what I mean. Up till now it's been me on top, me screwing you, and for once I want to be the one flat on my back.'

'I thought you liked –'

'Come on, be honest. It's no great deal, but I reckon you can't do it, can you? Like with the stutter, you're half stuck in there and you need someone to squeeze it out of you.'

'That's n-not f-fair. If y-you want that y-you should say.'

'Really? OK, let's start with a little tickle, eh?'

'What? Ow! No, d-don't, you're – oh, damn! Shit, Mouse, I've spilt the d-dope, get off, I –'

'Bollocks. We'll have to hold on anyway, Stray. McGinlay's appeared outside.'

Des walked out and felt a cool breeze on his forehead. He looked up. When darkness hits the city, the sky goes. A relief. Eyes can now be rooted to the ground, horizons lost behind ceilings of light. The sky is a distraction. It's a void or a reminder of somewhere else. Des didn't want to think of places beyond just yet; that could tempt fate and increase pressure when he was so close to the end. He looked over at the office towers with their grids of light. Thirty storeys of furtive labouring. People on the scale of ants. The way it goes, the way we are, thought Des, feeling weary once more, feeling the bruises beginning to ache. He physically tried to pull himself together and not to give in to dread. He saw a Bentley, silent and ominous, cruise towards him.

24

'The things we do, eh, McGinlay, for our employers.'

'I'm not working for mine any more.'

'Yeh, guess that's true.'

It wasn't exactly a fair situation. Des on his own backed up against a timetable board and the two of them, squat Ross and bulky Gus, standing a little way back by the Bentley. But Des wasn't going to complain; it could make them feel more at ease.

'So you admit that you work for Wainwright, then?'

'Nah, that's not really the situation, although he'd like to think it was. Associates, I say. I'm just doing the guy a favour trying to sort this business out.'

'Quite a favour.'

'That's business, McGinlay. A few favours here, a few deals there – confidence, self-interest. It's complicated but it all hangs together somehow.'

'You've lost me already.'

'Yeh, well, it's a different ball game, ain't it? I mean, you're just a self-employed grifter really, screwing what you can from people's problems, like Bertha for instance.'

'She got her money's worth out of me, I reckon.'

'I bet she did. Did you know I was shacked up with her once?'

'Yeh.'

'Quite a woman in her way. Went to seed, of course, but

she still had – what you call it? – "sexual charisma". Charm the pants off most men. Bet you had a fair taste.'

'Of course, you were immune.'

'The fuck I wasn't! I ended up in the nick because of her! Still, that's dead and buried now.'

'I wouldn't count on it. I mean, you did bump off her daughter.'

'Don't slip that shit in, man! She might've wanted to stitch me up for any number of reasons, but I don't reckon she will any more.'

'Huh-uh, you reckon?'

Ross suppressed a smile. 'Ever tried cleaning windows on the third floor?'

'What you on about?'

'Nothing, man, cept we've chewed the fat long enough and it's time we sorted this deal out.'

Des was beginning to wonder whether he could pull it off. Ross was the type who led with his mouth but nothing he said held any substance. Oil on seawater slopping around rocks and then slipping away again. But that was words for you, something to drown in, something to obscure action.

'So what are the basics of this conversation then, Ross?'

'What d'you mean?'

'Wainwright, when I first broached the subject, he seemed happy with a cash deal and maybe a bit of information too, but then he got peeved. Some victims of his own stupidity trashed his house, so then he says it's the photos or my neck. Not a good thing to say in the circumstances. I feel quite touchy about my neck.'

'Understandable,' Ross agreed. 'Threats of physical violence, they rub people up the wrong way. But, you know, Wainwright's an amateur. He loses his cool and you have to make allowances for that shit.'

'I don't want to make any allowances for that shit.'

'I know, but what the fuck, that's why I'm here and I can't see why a few thou your way shouldn't sort this problem out.'

'Sounds better. And a bit of information maybe, just to satisfy my own curiosity, you understand?'

'Come on, McGinlay. What information? My client, understandably, just wants to keep a few photos out of the public domain. There's nothing more to it than that.'

'That's got to be the understatement of the year.'

'That's the b-bloke!'

'You're sure, Stray?'

'I f-fucking well am! I saw him d-down the Lime, ponytail and p-part of a f-finger missing. M-Mary pulled him. She said he was m-more interested in whether she took d-dirty p-pictures than he was in her.'

'He certainly looks a slimebag, like one of those ageing rock stars from the seventies who thinks he's done it all.'

'Yeh, well, this b-bleeder probably has.'

'Don't worry, we've got surprise on our side. It's the black guy who worries me. Must be the minder. Don't know how we'll get round him.'

'D'you think we're b-being t-total idiots?'

'Ha, probably, but it's exciting. I feel totally aroused, Stray.'

'N-Not again.'

'Don't be so miserable. We're involved, right with the action and we have a righteous target standing out there.'

'And I b-bet that's as far as it g-gets. I hope McGinlay's g-going to do something about it.'

'Doesn't look like it, does it? Let's face it, Stray, that guy's just out there for the dosh.'

'Like everyone it seems.'

'God, you're such a bloody defeatist! Feel, for fuck sake! Feel the anger. Let's bleedin well do something for once!'

'I'm t-trying, Mouse, I really am t-trying.'

'OK, Ross, let's take this in easy stages. You said a few thou, how much exactly is that?'

'A deuce, and pretty good for you since it's a bonus. But I don't mind. You've seen an opportunity to play the market, you have a rare commodity and it's plain business sense to make as much as you can. But get this, McGinlay, that's as far as it goes.'

Des took a glance up at the towerblocks that surrounded them. As the meeting had progressed, the number of lights in the towers had diminished. People switching off, clocking off and going home. He briefly thought he'd like the certainty of that. To turn off the wire, grab his two thou and head for home. But then, where was that?

'OK, Ross, you're right,' he said. 'This is a bonus for me and I'll settle for that, but, well, there is an edge in this for me too, like Scobie Brent's claws around my neck.'

'Come on, McGinlay, you got your own back.'

Des then noticed big Gus stepping forward. He seemed irritated as he loomed over Ross's shoulder.

'Shit, boss, dis guy im jus stringing you along, an you know we gotta get places t'night.'

'Yeh, you're right, man. Come on, McGinlay, let's do the exchange and get the fuck out of here. You're wasting time.'

'OK, but you know, just for me, Scobie was the one who killed Claudette, right?'

'Jesus, McGinlay.'

'It's no big deal for you, is it? You said the guy had to go.'

Ross stood back a little and put his hands on his hips. He looked around briefly at the straggling passengers heading for the station.

'OK. Let me put you straight about Scobie, right. The geezer's an arsehole, but occasionally in the past I have used the guy, as an errand boy, a bodyguard – for shipping cash to the bank, delivering cars – you know. He's a tough nut and provides good protection.'

'What is all this shit?' Des couldn't help but notice that Gus was edging closer. Like clouds approaching the sun, Gus was a shadow blotting out streetlight.

'What I'm saying, McGinlay, is that Scobie is a casual. He did work for lots of guys, maybe even Wainwright.'

'That sounds total crap to me.'

'You said you wanted information. Fuck knows whether he killed Claudette. All I know is I heard Wainwright cussing Scobie off, said he shouldn't leave his spunk up a dead girl's cunt.'

'I bet Wainwright would be interested in you saying –'

It was the full eclipse. Des suddenly lost sight of light as a half-smiling Gus leaned over. There was malice in his eyes and garlic on his breath.

'Reckon I owe you one, arsehole.'

'Piss off.'

'You got one over me the udder night. Man, I reckon it's repay time.'

A slab of hand attached itself to Des's jacket. The Perspex cover of the timetable board shuddered as Des backed into it. Another slab hand began to delve roughly into places Des regarded as private.

'Call this lump off, Ross, and let's finish the bloody deal.'

'You're too curious, McGinlay, that's your problem.'

'Fuck me, you were dead right, boss. Dis guy's gotta lickle black box.'

'OK, get the photo stuff and let's split, and quick before anyone else comes!'

Gus's slab hands found brown manila but they couldn't quite get a grip. Something else made a connection. A kneecap got uppity and crushed into a groin. Gus's great shadow swayed back just a little, Des saw a brief flicker of streetlight but not enough. There was no room to swing a punch. It was arms around each other time, vindictive hugs. Like a drunken sumo dance, Des and Gus staggered together, straining for imbalance and a decisive trip. Ross Constanza saw immediately that he didn't carry the weight to sort out such a tangle. He quickly stepped back to the Bentley, put his hand inside and brought out the gun.

The battered blue van revved up raucously. The gear stick had a violent fit until Mouse's podgy hand calmed it down. Jerry put his hands up to his ears. He looked around in panic before putting his own hand over Mouse's.

'W-W-What are you d-doing?'

'This is our chance, Stray.'

'B-But, w-what d-do you m-mean?'

'Look, they're all over the shop. They won't notice us.'

'B-But w-what are we g-going t-to d-do?' Jerry almost screamed out the words, and he knew he was shaking far more than the gear stick. Sweat slicked his brow, and he had a dreadful feeling inside, one that he'd felt only twice before.

'Justice, Stray, it's fucking out there staring us in the face, and we're going to take it, grab our destiny, vent our bloody anger!'

With those words, Mouse wrenched the gear stick into place and slammed her foot down. The van lurched forward, slewed reluctantly to the right, banged into a parked car, mounted the pavement and then went straight for the fracas ahead.

'M-Mouse, I'm gonna be sick. I'm g-gonna p-pass out.'

'Here comes retrib –!' Mouse shouted.

The van slammed straight into the back of Gus. He and Des shot forward and crashed against the timetable board. Ross, having a few seconds warning, dived to the side. The van missed him by inches but the wing mirror didn't. A solid crack on the head, the mirror bent backwards and

Ross slumped forward into the open door of the battered van. A shocked Jerry saw the ponytail drape over his shoe and he felt nausea well up once again.

'Is that the bastard who got Mary? Is that him?'

'Y-Yeh.'

'Pull him inside!'

'Wha –?'

'Come on! Grab him! There's people coming! Grab his belt and hold on!'

Once again a podgy hand hit the gears, a Doc Marten stamped down with rage and the battered blue van hurtled off into the night.

25

The nurse was nice. It was as if she really cared, that Des was special, that he could reach out from his lousiness and hug that uniform which was so sexy because it wasn't supposed to be. As he eased his way down the corridor with her holding his arm, he almost believed this was his true reward and they were on the way to Las Palmas.

'You want me to call you a taxi?'

The downer. Come up for coffee, yes, but don't expect to stay. Des heaved a big sigh. *Just like always . . . what she's paid to do.*

'It's OK, a friend's gonna pick me up. Park me in the waiting room and I'll be fine.' And he was fine. A little winded, a bit groggy, but not a broken bone or scratch on his skin. Big Gus had been a buffer, a human airbag, and after the check-up, Des was declared unharmed. Sad for Gus that he had a broken pelvis and severe concussion. But maybe not too sad. Des felt the van might've fared worse. Errol was already in the waiting room. He gave Des a 'here we go again' look and strolled over.

'I can take over from here, nurse. Is he OK?'

'Just shaken up that's all. He needs rest and should watch out for signs of delayed reaction.'

'Well, I guess I can handle that for him.'

Des groaned to himself. He somehow thought he was in the doghouse.

'So how is it then, Errol, the state of things?'

'Messy, real messy, of the bucketful of shit kind.'

'Thought it might be.'

Errol eased his Audi into the traffic crawl that led to Argent Street. Rain was beginning to fall. The windscreen became a gleaming gem-case and the city outside was a slurry of light. Des eased back in his seat. He didn't want to talk about the case, he didn't care any more. All Des wanted was some soul slush from the CD, a few thoughts about Pearl and a nice joint so that the lights outside would make music too. Errol wasn't going to oblige.

'Come on, Des, what d'you know about the Ross abduction? I mean, him and that blue van have disappeared into thin air.'

'They took him away!'

'What d'you mean, "they"?'

'I didn't get much of a look, but I guess it was Jerry Coton and some of his anarchist friends.'

'What?'

'You know, the guy who was having it off with Mary.' Des looked over at Errol and didn't like the view. He quickly went on talking. 'Well, this Jerry guy, he did stutter something about revenge. I reckon, some drop-out gits from the squat he'd shacked up in, they did some sort of guerrilla attack on Wainwright's place.'

'Eh? Des, why do I always get totally lost when I talk to you about this case? How would some spoilt white trash end up at the meet we had arranged? What the hell's going on, Des?'

'I did sort of mention it. They're just half-crazy dopeheads that's all.'

'Je-sus!'

'Don't worry, they'll turn up.'

'Yeh, they'll possibly turn up dead.'

'Nah. Ross'll probably thank them for rescuing him. He'll probably give them the money I almost had my fingers on, the bastard. Shit, you haven't got a spliff, have you, Errol?'

As they drove on, silence commenced, and accumulated. The calm-before-the-storm kind of silence that, as Des knew, the longer it went on, the greater the inevitable outburst. Des tried some pre-emptive charm.

'Yeh, can't agree with you more, Errol. It was a balls-up. Ross was slippery and well clued up; he was covering himself all the time. What could I do? But there was some loose talk surely, enough to get them all in for questioning?'

Errol kissed his teeth and stayed silent for a few minutes longer.

'All right, Des, the wire wasn't so bad as far as it went,' he said. 'A finger was put on Scobie and we can do all the forensic stuff and maybe nobble the shit. But the rest is totally dicey, Des. I told you, Wainwright has influence. They're not going to act on that, especially with the way it all turned out. And I ain't gonna push, man. There's already a big dent in my promotion.'

'Yeh, well, I guess I expected that, which is why I sent off some stuff to the local paper.'

'What?'

'Put all the blame on me, Errol. A loose cannon, an unregulated free enterprise PI, a stubborn and stupid dickhead. Feel free. I don't want to hurt you. I'm thinking of fucking off to the Canary Isles anyway.'

'Not just yet, brother. You've got to help me find Ross. Those little innuendoes on the tape? Bertha Turton is dead, Des, and that bastard seemed to know it!'

*　　*　　*

Someone had wiped the names off the map. Jerry didn't

know where he was. Several hours they'd been driving and he'd finally managed to get Mouse to take a break. All he could see was darkness, and the dots and threaded lines of lights on a black page. Jerry had ceased to believe in landscapes. All he knew was he stood outside and a lousy wind blew in his face. He looked uneasily back to the van. The 'bad guy' was in there. They had to decide what to do with him. Mouse's idea was to drive to the sea and dump the guy in. 'Simple,' she said. Like hell it was. Mouse had a thing about the sea. A complete opposite to the city. A deep and wild place where the curve of the planet can always be seen. A place that makes you feel small but never downtrodden. Fine, but where was it? Whichever way you drive in England, she said, you always reach the sea. *Yeh, great, unless you drive around in circles.* Jerry lit a fag and made his own mark on the black page. He knew what was happening, he knew he wanted to back out. He kicked his feet restlessly. His hardly smoked fag fizzled into the hedge like a shooting star. Back to a black page. He went to the rear door of the van and opened it. Ross was splayed out on the mattress with arms and legs tied to the sides of the van. Jerry looked at the sack that covered his face and guessed he could probably be seen through it. But Ross didn't move and he couldn't speak because his gob was taped. What now? Jerry sighed and then reluctantly went to Mouse in the front cab.

'I just looked in on the b-bad guy.'

'I heard.'

'He didn't move a m-muscle.'

'Maybe he's had a heart attack.'

'I d-didn't think of that.'

'I hope he hasn't. Not after coming this far.'

Jerry sighed again. Mouse was counting out the money they'd found. The gun was stuffed in the waistband of her leggings and a half-smoked joint balanced on her lower lip.

221

'So? Come on then, what wonderful ideas did the fresh air give you?'

'C-Can't say I g-got m-many, M-Mouse.'

'You got some, though?'

'I dunno . . .'

It wasn't fair, Jerry thought. Mouse, she was just like any other down-and-out really, but she was so bright. She had a mind like a knife. He was all right with her most of the time, could ease along nicely and make believe that he didn't stutter. But then, when she unsheathed her blade, he was stumbling over his tongue like a blind man on rocks.

'I m-mean, well, you know I hate the shit, d-despise him. I m-mean, I'm really g-glad we've got this far . . .'

'Got cold feet eh, Stray?'

'I dunno, I c-can't . . .'

He tried to hold his own and look her in the eye. Blue eyes, clear and lucid, they sat in her face like jewels in a battered casket. Yes, Mouse was showing signs of wear and tear. Worry lines and the beginnings of a double chin. Suddenly, Jerry began to feel horny and he thought that it wasn't such a bad idea.

'So what is it then, M-Mouse? What is it that m-makes you so – v-vindictive? It's l-like you want to get your own b-back m-more than me.'

Jerry eased in close and rested his hand on the dome of her belly.

'I don't think you'd understand.'

'C-Come on, I've t-told you stuff about me.'

Jerry began to edge his hand down her belly. Like always, it was exciting and Mouse didn't seem to mind.

'A lot of people say I've got a chip on my shoulder, a mean streak or whatever. I usually say back to them that it's hardly surprising given the shit that's around.'

Jerry moved his hand down to her legs, the bad guy and the crappy van fast disappearing from his thoughts.

'I don't understand it myself, cept I feel some sort of fear and want to kick out all the time. There's this image I keep seeing, a darkened room and a tall dark shadow coming towards me. I don't know who or when or what but I know that shadow means pain.'

As Jerry's hand began to move between her legs, Mouse suddenly grabbed it.

'Don't do that!' Her eyes narrowed and she began to bend his fingers back.

'M-Mouse, I w-was only – ow!'

'Shall we try and sort out what to do?'

'OK, OK.'

Mouse let go.

'Why d-don't we just leave him, d-dump him by the road? That could be g-good, with a n-note to the p-police saying he's a murderer. It'd b-be enough for me. We'll have m-made our point.'

'You're just trying to justify doing nothing.'

'So what the b-bloody hell d-do you want to do?'

Mouse stared out into the darkness. Jerry thought she seemed different: not so concerned about him, wrapped up in herself. This was worrying. He didn't know where he was. He was totally dependent on her. Mouse relit her spliff.

'I've just realized, we've got that shitty guy back there and we can do whatever we want.'

'Yeh?'

'Think of the power of it, Stray. We're not the victims.'

Jerry looked out at the night with its restless wind and emptiness. He couldn't think of anything except that he was trapped. He then heard a little sob from Mouse and saw that her eyes were wet.

'I was just thinking of all the millions of animals that have been killed out here, in the country, all those dumb victims we're not supposed to feel anything for.'

'Oh no, M-Mouse, d-don't – don't let it g-get to you.'

'I guess you're right. You can't think about it, can you? It's impossible to absorb. You have to be hard.'

'Or just l-let it g-go.'

'No, I think there is something, something I can try to do.'

Mouse pulled out the gun and shuffled on her knees into the back of the van. The sack was wrenched from Ross's face and his cold eyes blinked.

'Hello, fucker,' she said, giggling and then wobbling her breasts in his face. She showed him the gun. Ross began to move. He writhed in a taut kind of way and there was a muffled sound from his mouth. Mouse pointed the gun straight between his eyes. Jerry winced and shut his. He waited, but nothing happened.

'Look at him, Stray. He's nothing now, just a useless shit.'

'A m-murdering shit.'

'And a pile of other bad things, no doubt.'

Jerry kicked Ross's leg and then wished he hadn't. He didn't want to encourage Mouse.

'I used to have this fantasy once about the Prime Minister. It sounds daft I know, but I imagined I was part of this underground group who managed to take him hostage. We didn't want any money. We just wanted revenge for all the nastiness inflicted by the state. So I'd imagine ways to abuse, demean and torture the bastard.'

'Yeh, well those s-sort, they're un-t-touchable, like that rich p-prick who started all this.'

'It's feeling helpless and wanting to hit back.' Mouse looked over at Jerry. 'But we're not helpless now, are we?'

'C-Come on, M-Mouse, let's –'

'I think we need some kind of ceremony. A ritual or something, you know, to celebrate what we've got here and see what comes out.'

'I w-want a j-joint.'

'Roll one then and I'll see what else I can find.'

224

Mouse shuffled back to the cab and Jerry remained, fumbling for his rolling gear. Ross was looking at him. Sweat glistened around his eyes and it seemed as if he was appealing to Jerry's masculine nature. Well, he wasn't going to have any of that. Ross was disgusting. Ross screwed Mary and then had her killed. Jerry'd be glad to see the back of him. He could hardly feel an inch of sympathy. Mouse came back.

'This is all I could find.' She was carrying a couple of cans of engine oil, a bag of crisps and the gun. 'What's that stuff they shove in your mouth in church?'

'Eh?'

'Never mind . . .'

Mouse moved across the mattress. She kneeled down between the bad guy's splayed legs and took her leggings down. Jerry found himself staring at her bare bum, pumpkin bum. She then took off her T-shirt and flaunted herself at Ross.

'Look at me, you scumbag. I am Mary and all the other women you've abused.'

She prodded him in the ribs with the gun, then reached over and picked up a can of oil.

This is weird, thought Jerry. Then, seeing her bent down like that, he began to get excited again. He forgot the joint and started taking his own clothes off.

'I wish I had the words to go with this.' Mouse opened the oilcan and held it over Ross. 'You know, Stray, like you get with weddings and funerals. But nothing's –'

'Deliver us from the shits of this world so we can all live in peace,' Jerry muttered, as he struggled out of the clothes.

'That's nice, Stray. Yes, spit on their faces.'

Mouse did spit and then tipped oil onto Ross's face. Jerry finally managed to get out of his clothes. Kneeling on the mattress, he got behind Mouse. 'Deliver us from normality that we may live again,' he said.

'God, Stray, you're pretty good with words, and you're not stuttering either.'

Mouse poured more oil, smeared some on herself and took a few bitefuls of crisps. Jerry began to run his hands over her smooth back.

'This is revenge for all that pain and all that abuse,' she declared.

More oil was splashed and the proddings of the gun got more violent. Jerry hoped it wouldn't go off. But he was losing interest in all that, he was manoeuvring her legs apart and savouring the moistness that lay within. Mouse had picked up another can of oil.

'With this – oh!'

Jerry could delay his entry no longer. It seemed the only compulsion then, maybe the last one, and he wanted to lose himself in it for ever. The oil went all over the place. No more words from Mouse and no more proddings from the gun. Jerry was as happy as he'd ever been amid the grunts and the slime and the naked flesh, fucking for all he was worth, doggy style.

*   *   *

'Can't prove much on this one,' Errol said as he looked at the open window in Bertha's flat. 'Unless we get some witnesses.'

Des looked at the window, the smear of window cleaner on the glass and the bottle on the sill. Most of all he looked at the pale pink curtains and the frilly pelmet. He shivered.

'It'd be dead easy to set up. Maybe a punch to her jaw, lift her up and throw her out. Put the window-cleaning stuff out after.'

'She could've just fell,' Des murmured. 'I reckon she had her mind on other things and that can make you careless.'

'She was dressed up to the nines, Des.'

226

'Any sign of cash or photos?'

'Nah, even more suspicious, eh?'

Des looked around the room. Pink paper flowers, the flouncy bits on the shelving, the doilies and cute ornaments. He averted his eyes from the bedroom door. That was the place he didn't want to see. That was the womb, the last succouring place before the desert; that was Bertha alive and bringing life to Des.

'So you reckon Ross had any reason to kill her?'

'Probably. She was up to something, calling me off. Maybe that was it. She'd got a lever out of me and wanted to prise open some blood money, get a bit of revenge for Claudette and past sins against her.'

'Which is why we need to find Ross.'

'Or get Gus to talk.'

'Yeh. Though I'm sure both options'll be useless without evidence.'

'It's a sad end.'

'They always are, man. Come on, I'll drive you home.'

Des tried not to think about it. Carnal knowledge and death. The uneasiness fretted away all the same. Hot passionate flesh, cold dead flesh. Ecstasy and expiration. His first big job and he'd got too close. He'd made every mistake that you could. Bertha could end up haunting him for a very long time.

'So what's the silence about then, Des?'

Errol was trying to get his car across Argent Street and into Des's road. The traffic had eased, but the speed of vehicles going past was greater. It was dodgy just to nose the car out.

'Dunno. Too many deaths I guess.'

'I reckon you quite liked Bertha.'

'Sort of. I mean, she was a right manipulative sod but, you know, she did things that made you feel good. She had something . . .'

227

'A fair enough epitaph.'

Errol finally got across Argent Street and down to Des's home.

'OK, you gotta rest up, Des, an watch out for any signs of delayed concussion or whatever. So no booze, eh brother, an non a dat dere devil weed! OK?'

'Sure thing, Doc. I'm just gonna count my money and see if it was worth it.'

Des didn't do any counting that night. And the booze and ganja got well tapped. Of course, it wasn't actually anything, it was just a start, an aspiration – but all the same, she was a cracker and he had almost felt the sand between his toes. The note he'd had through the door got obliterated but it read something like this:

Dear Des

Bad news. I'm sorry but Carlos got physical tonight and I've quit. You'll know the only way I can quit is by leaving. By the time you get this, that's what I'll have done. I'm on my way to Las Palmas. It would be great if you could follow me. Sorry again, lover. I'm missing you.

Love, Pearl

*   *   *

They'd been travelling ages since the last stop and still there was no sign of the sea. Jerry had seen plenty of roads, empty towns and endless features of landscape made weird by headlights.

'You sure you know what you're doing?' Jerry had moaned.

'Don't worry, I'll get us there. I know my way around.'

The van was on its last legs. The engine groaned, rattled

228

and struggled to take the slightest rise. There was an acrid smell in the cab, too, mingling with the oil that came from everywhere. Jerry was feeling sick and his nausea wasn't helped by Mouse's erratic driving. As Jerry looked through the darkness at the flashing white lines, he felt he was on a rope being swung from side to side. He wished she'd stop.

'Did you read that thing in the papers, Jerry, about that bloke who ran someone over? He was so pissed off with the woman he'd hit, he turned his car round and ran over her again.'

'Shit, no!'

'True. And this bloke, he got off on some crap charge. A few months in nick. Told some bullshit story about how his wife was leaving him, his job was on the line, he was late for work, been stuck in traffic jams – blah, blah – said he just snapped when he hit the woman. "Mitigating circumstances," the judge called it.'

'Typical judge.'

'Says it all. If you want to kill someone, just get in your car and run them over, then plead mitigating circumstances.'

'Cars and property, the gods of today.'

'Gives us a let-out, though, eh? Mitigating circumstances, after what the bad guy did to your woman.'

'Yeh, but what're we going to do with him, Mouse?'

The van hit another rise in the road and seriously struggled. It just managed to make it to the top before the engine croaked and fizzled out. Mouse eased the van over to the verge and stopped.

'Shit!'

'Now what?'

With the van lights out, total darkness loomed ahead of them. Not a dot or a gleam anywhere, not a star twinkling in the sky. Mouse slid open the van door and let her legs dangle out in the cool air.

'S'pose I could take a look.'

'God, I've n-never seen such darkness. Never g-get it in the city, do you?'

'Open your door, Stray. Have a sniff. I can smell the sea, you know.'

Jerry did so and he could smell the sea. And, as his eyes got used to the dark, he thought he could see it too. There was a bumpy open field close by. But then, far off, beneath greyish clouds, there was blackness that seemed to move like a seething snake flecked with glimmers of light.

'Look over there,' he said to Mouse. 'You reckon that's it?'

'Yeh. I think we've made it, Stray.'

Mouse got out of the van and walked to the edge of the grass. With her hands on her hips, she took in great gulps of air and held her head up to the clouds. Jerry thought she looked pretty imposing. He began to think again about how he could stop her doing something drastic. The last time had merely postponed matters. But he didn't really know what to do and hated being reliant on her. He just wanted rid of Ross and the whole messy venture. He didn't like the empty darkness and the cold wind. The name Jerry was beginning to mean something again. He had lost his stutter and was feeling homesick for the city. Mouse lumbered her way back into the van.

'Well, the sea's down there somewhere, but I can't tell how far.'

'Come on, Mouse, what shall we do with this guy?'

'You still feeling squeamish?'

'Yeh, s'pose so. I just want to get away from here. I don't like it.'

'Well, I definitely want to go down to the beach.'

'Oh yeh. How do we do that? This van's fucked.'

'We can freewheel it down, it can't be far now.'

Jerry groaned to himself. Mouse had become so intense

and stubborn about this sea thing and all he wanted was a spliff and a nice warm bed. He didn't seem to have a say in anything any more.

'So let's at least dump the bad guy? We could leave a note or something, like I said.'

'After coming this far?'

'God, Mouse, you've just hijacked the whole bloody thing. It was supposed to be my revenge, remember?'

'And you've just been trying to stop me from doing what I want . . . all those snidey sex games.'

'I don't want to end up in the nick.'

'Oh, sod it, you're just whingeing.'

Mouse suddenly grabbed the handbrake and thrust it down. She rocked impatiently in her seat. Slowly the van began to move.

'Bloody hell, Mouse, I think we should –'

'I got us this far; I'll get us all the way.'

They began to pick up speed. Apart from the creaks of the van, the only noise was a wind which moaned and roared. Jerry began to feel more and more angry. She was doing it again, taking over. The road ahead, going ever down, began to curve and bend. Mouse seemed to be enjoying the ride, her shoulders heaving at each deviation in the road.

'I think we should stop this, Mouse. It's dangerous.'

'We're going to the sea!'

'Jesus, we could get out and walk, I'm sure.'

It was all becoming too much. Jerry, feeling sick with the motion, was genuinely scared as the van's headlights swerved through the dark. He didn't want this and he was furious with Mouse.

'Stop it!'

'Too late, Stray.'

Mouse pulled the van sharply to the right and they screeched onto a straighter stretch of road. The sea was clearly visible now. Jerry grabbed the steering wheel.

'Come on, Mouse, pull over.'

'Sod you!'

Mouse tried to dislodge Jerry's hand. He tried to pull right and force the van onto a grassy verge. The van began to swerve back and forth across the road.

'Fuck! Fuck you, Jerry!'

Mouse glared at him and then violently wrenched the steering wheel to the left. Jerry lost his grip. The van bumped off the road and onto a slope. The sea was ahead of them, a misty glow in the night.

'God, Mouse, put the brakes on!'

'Sod you.'

26

They'd renamed the place. It was the Fedora no more. Des now pushed through the doors of the Spit and Shovel. Of course, it could've been the wrong place entirely. The outside location was hardly distinctive. Des began to feel that way when he saw the rough plastered walls and black beams where there should've been palms and Bogart eyes. Only Wayne's stubbled face gave Des hope that he was in the right place. He went in further, noting pickaxes, peat spades and heavy-duty hammers clamped to the walls. The place was also half busy. Young white men mostly, office juniors knocking back the latest trend in beers. Feeling distinctly uncomfortable, Des made it to the bar and managed to catch Wayne's eye.

'Jesus, Wayne, what's going on?'

'Fuck knows.'

'I thought I'd walked into the wrong place.'

'The bleedin brewery for you. Retro working class or something. Aiming for the lads who've never done a hard day's work in their life but whose dads did, or some such crap as that.'

'At least you're quite busy.'

'We do live bands now. Got a gig on later, some loud fart called Stevie Kitson. So, what you having then, mate?'

'A coupla doubles of whisky.'

'My, doing well, are we?'

'I've made a few bob.'

'Your mate's over in the corner.'

'Great. Any phone calls?'

'Yeh, a couple of numbers I can give you. Maybe work in it.'

'Even better.' Des smiled. 'So, Wayne, tell me, how long you reckon this name's gonna stick?'

Wayne smiled back, and then they both said it.

'Fuck knows!'

Errol was up to his peanut routine, only this time he had them laid out on the table in circle form. He had his shoulders hunched and didn't look too happy.

'I reckon you're ten peanuts earlier than your usual lateness.'

'There's an improvement for you.'

'You were right about this place. It doesn't exist. It's a virtual reality. I mean, will you look at this crap?'

Des did. Behind Errol there was a photo of a guy with a walrus moustache sitting on a huge anchor chain. To the right, the blackened face of a miner stared down. A collection of miner's lamps was stuffed on a shelf above him.

'We're only a few steps away. They'll be changing the scenery every night.'

'Too right. So how was the funeral?'

'Grim. A couple of workmates, a few neighbours and me. Oh, and this Paddy Conroy geezer standing well away at the back.'

'Bertha's final bad deal.'

'Yeh, buried next to her daughter. Two chancers who took the hard way out.'

'It's been one hell of a messy case.'

It had been, and there were still things left unresolved. Scobie had been charged with Claudette's murder but he refused to admit any involvement. The word was the shrinks were parcelling him up for the funny farm. It seems Scobie was raving on about being the reincarnation of a lion. He was the 'Lord of the Jungle'. Des's hammer might have had something to do with that. Sir Martin Wainwright had left the country. The press published the allegations. The police said they would investigate, but it all seemed to have fizzled out. 'On a long business trip,' said Sir Martin's personal assistant, 'and we don't know when he'll be back.' No more political high hopes for him then. And it was nearly a week before Ross's body was found. The battered blue van had gone over a cliff and been half covered with tumbling rocks. Down in Dorset, some fossil hunter found it, and Ross, a strung-up form covered with feeding crabs. But there was no sign of Jerry or his friend Mouse, and they still hadn't turned up. Probably gone checking out weed in the ocean, stoned, drifting and hoping to be Atlantis-bound. Loose ends, all over the place.

'So, man, you haven't made it to the Canary Isles yet?'

'Haven't been much further than the end of my road.'

'You should go, man.'

'I'm working up to it, but, you know, I've just felt too weary, too flattened out to even lift a finger.'

'Well, I did say, didn't I, man, that job and you being out on your own, there's no clocking off like with me. Your sort of position, it goes through the front door, through you and on, deep. You get eaten up, burnt out.'

'Guess I should go and seek Pearl, long shot that it is.'

'Yeh. You won't be up to your necks in shit this time.'

'And what a lot of shit we had. I mean, Errol, now, it's hard to see what the fuss was about.'

'What you mean?'

'Sex.'

'Sex? It's what you do when you aren't working. Sometimes . . . if you're lucky.'

'Yeh, but going to those lengths for a bit of kinkiness, doing murder for Christ's sake!'

'I guess it's all about the buzz of it. Like drugs, man, you always need to go further to get the same fix. For some screwballs, murder must be the ultimate.'

'Maybe that's what was with Scobie, but Wainwright?'

'Power, I guess. When you're right up there in the clouds, you don't have to face the reality of the decisions you take. A bit of lechery goes wrong – what's he care what Scobie did?'

'He shouldn't have needed to get anything done. Getting caught with a whore, who cares?' Des shivered inside. Somehow, all the rationalizing didn't sound convincing.

'You and me don't give two fucks, but this country, man, it still got a tight-arsed establishment that demands respect. They might screw donkeys in their spare time, but it just ain't acceptable that anybody should know.'

Des eased back in his seat and downed the last of his whisky. The booze was working. About time. He could feel it sizzle in his veins, and see it too in Errol, in that sudden flush on his face.

'Yeh, well I reckon it's definitely Las Palmas for me then.'

'Des.' Errol looked him squarely in the eyes. 'Go there.'

JAKARTA SHADOWS

Alan Brayne

Jakarta, Indonesia. The city is edgy after the fall of Soeharto, the country engulfed in religious strife and urban violence. Most westerners have fled. Not rootless, disenchanted Graham Young.

But after a skin-crawling encounter at the Hotel Platinum, Graham is caught up in a sex-killings investigation. As Jakarta closes in, he becomes further alienated from the sterile comforts of ex-pat life. Gin's soft focus eludes him and terror surfaces even on cloudless Bali.

Sidestepping sinister forces, Graham slides from a glitzy mall buzzing with would-be rich to the Moonbeam for pool games with 'butterflies of the night'. A thumbprint in blood and malevolent interrogation ratchet up his paranoia. And around every corner lurk corruption and dread.

'A sense of unease permeates this atmospheric thriller, set in unstable Indonesia, where nothing is what it seems, and no one can be trusted. The plot twists and turns, taking in murder, betrayal and corruption before reaching its unsettling conclusion.' *Christopher Harris*

ISBN: 0 9535895 8 7